Also by J. Anthony Castagno

———

Octavia and the Greek Key

Dance of the Red Panel

The Fugitive Series - Coming in early 2016

Witness to Terror

Out of Tunis

THE LADY OF THE LANTERN

J. Anthony Castagno
A Novella

This is a work of fiction. All characters, businesses, places, events or incidents either are the products of the author's imagination or used in a fictitious manner. Any resemblance to actual persons, living or dead, or actual events is purely coincidental.

Good can exist without evil, whereas evil cannot exist without good.

Thomas Aquinas

Chapter I

THE LADY STRIKES

Laura smiled as Ed guided the car up the narrow two-lane road beside the Panama Canal's Gatun Locks. Out on their third date, his father had let him take the family's new 1965 red Chevy Impala for the first time. When the car reached the edge of Gatun Lake, he turned onto a single-lane dirt road running along the edge of the water. The short road ended at a secluded plot of grass adjacent dense jungle. The kids at school knew the spot well. They named it Parker's Place.

Ed stopped the car facing the lake, twenty feet from the water's dark slate surface. He turned off the engine and lights and pushed the seat back.

Laura loved this spot. The full moon hung high on the horizon and its mirror image reflected off the still water. She slid to the middle of the bench seat. Ed put an arm over her shoulder and pulled her close. They kissed and Laura placed her arms around his neck. His hand slid under her shirt and to her breast.

Laura gently pushed him away and frowned. "Stop." After a deep breath, she leaned her head against the seat. The moon, floating above the lake, drew her eyes.

Ed touched her arm. "Sorry. You know we don't have to go all the way."

"Let's not to start something we can't stop."

He lifted a damp cloth from the dashboard and wiped his face and neck. From the floorboard, he raised a paper bag. "Want more rum and coke?"

"No."

Laura placed her hands in her lap and stared out the windshield. Movement in the grass, outside the open window beside her, caught her attention. Without looking at Ed, she poked his leg and raised a finger to her lips. She pointed at three coatimundis in the grass. The small creatures reminded her of tan raccoons with long pointed snouts. A mother led a procession of two coatimundi babies toward the jungle. "Stay behind me."

She pushed open her door and kneeled behind it. Ed slid across the seat, got out, and squatted, leaning against her back.

The mother coati alerted, chased her mini clan to the edge of the bush and they disappeared into a thick wall of vegetation.

"Hurry," Laura whispered. She stood, pulled Ed to the edge of the jungle and lowered herself to her knees. A few of her friends had caught coati babies and raised them as pets. *I'd love to have one.*

Ed touched her shoulder. "I don't think the mother will let us get close. Be careful. Her claws and teeth are sharp and she'll fight to protect those little guys."

"I will. I want to hold one."

"They're probably gone by now," Ed said.

Laura's shoulders drooped, and she looked into the jungle where the animals disappeared. "Here babies, come out."

As Ed strolled along the edge of the thick tangle and looked for the little creatures, he and Laura heard a branch snap. He looked at her and raised his eyebrows. "They must have moved this way."

Laura ran to his side. "Look in there, maybe the mother left one."

Ed knelt and parted the undergrowth with both hands. A few feet above his head, a branch moved and leaves rustled. He raised his head.

The vegetation in front of him erupted. A large black jaguar paw lashed from the dark wall of plants. Claws ripped open his exposed throat and severed a carotid artery. Blood gushed from his neck and painted the vegetation red.

Laura screamed and leapt back. Her mouth slackened and her eyes widened.

A second paw flashed forward and ripped flesh from Ed's chest, knocking him to his back.

Laura's knees gave out, and she dropped beside him. Her lips trembled seconds before her body started to shake. She wrapped her arms around her waist and whimpered at the sight of Ed's wide unfocused eyes and torn flesh. Her face contorted, and a scream stuck in her throat. Laura moved her eyes from him, staggered to her feet and took off toward the car. Halfway, her vision blurred, and she fell to the grass.

Chapter II

O'GRADY

Alisa sat on the couch in her pajamas and watched her husband, Canal Zone Police Detective Dan Casey, stop pacing and wipe perspiration from his face with a dishtowel. He continued his trek around the tropical rattan furniture in the living room.

A small air conditioner, hanging in a louvered window covered with plastic, fought a losing battle to cool the large room. The floor fan humming below it provided little help. *I can't stand it. We need a larger unit.*

Since the day she met him, eighteen years ago, Dan had changed little. Time had not softened the tough New Englander and proud product of Irish immigrant parents. She smiled to herself when remembering how she convinced him that a hard-nosed Irishman would blend in well with a Panamanian family. She chuckled.

"What did you say?" Dan asked.

"Nothing."

Dan strode across the room, opened the door, and gazed into the dark front yard at the bottom of the fifteen-foot high concrete staircase. Pushing the door closed he spun around, glanced at his watch and tapped the crystal. "What time is it Alisa?"

Now he has me worried. "It's three thirty. Ten minutes later than the last time you asked."

Dan stopped in the center of the room and focused on a leprechaun figurine, beside a telephone, on a table against the wall. "Damn it O'Grady. Where the hell is she?" He stared at the figurine as if awaiting a response.

"Dan," Alisa said and waited for him to answer. "Dan!"

"Sorry babe," he said as he walked to the couch and sat beside her.

"What did the dispatcher say?"

"The men on patrol are keeping their eyes out for her."

Alisa placed a hand on his arm. "Carol's never done this, it's the first time. She may have fallen asleep at a friend's house."

"I don't give a damn; she's grounded for this one. You told her to be home by eleven. That was four and a half hours ago." He looked at his cutoff sweat pants and pulled off his undershirt. "That's it. No reason to wait around any longer. I'm going out to look for her."

"You'll be going to work in three hours. What can you do that isn't being done?"

"I don't know, go to work and spend the next three hours driving around searching for her," he said leaving the room.

No matter what she said to him, he wouldn't listen. The best thing to do was let him go and they could contact each other through the dispatcher.

The telephone rang. Alisa leapt to the small table and snatched the handset from the phone. "Hello," she listened a moment and raised her eyes.

Dan ran into the room and she flashed him the OK sign.

"You know better than to do that. Your father and I worried ourselves to death."

Dan stepped beside her. "Where is she?"

Alisa raised her hand in front of his face and listened to her daughter for another moment. "Okay, be home by ten." She hung up and wrapped her arms around her husband. "She's at Katy's house. The beach made them tired, and they both fell asleep. It was an accident, don't be mad at her."

Dan shook his head. "I'll try, but she needs to be more responsible. Sometimes I worry too much."

Alisa kissed him. "That's why we love you. Just talk with her, she'll understand."

Chapter III

THE FISHING HOLE

Lou DeRosa, at six feet and one hundred and ninety pounds was solid and strong for a man in his mid-sixties. After spending most of his life in the Canal Zone, he retired a few months earlier. The simple things in life, fishing, hunting and drinking lots of beer, would fill the remaining days he had on earth.

Lou drove up the well-lit road running alongside Gatun Locks on his way to his favorite early morning fishing hole. The sun had not lifted above the horizon, but the color of the sky told him it would only be a few more minutes. He would have the bait bucket in the lake and a shrimp on a hook before the fiery ball broke over the jungle treetops.

The old pickup turned onto a dirt road leading to the grassy area a hundred yards from the locks. Two of his finest fishing poles overhung the truck bed. Glancing at the poles in his rear-view mirror, he grinned. *Lucky poles... lucky day.*

Near the end of the road, he spotted the red Impala. He stopped beside it, turned off the lights and cut the engine. His twelve-year-old truck had seen better days. The humid air and tropical rains had done their damage. The motor always started as soon as he turned the key, but each time he turned it off, the engine coughed more than a young boy inhaling his first stale Cuban cigar. He slid an open can of beer onto the dash and climbed out.

Lou stared at the Impala. *Why is Robinson's new car here this early?* Doc Robinson was not an early morning person, and not a fisherman. Lou once heard him say pulling and filling teeth made him enough money to buy all the fresh fish he wanted. Lou raised a hand to his chin and stared at the Impala. *This is odd.* He walked around the car and looked in the open windows. The keys were in the ignition and a half full rum bottle and coke bottle lay on the front seat. Lou scrunched his eyebrows and shook his head. Besides not fishing, Doc did not drink.

Light rapidly overtook the night darkness. He turned from the car and looked to the tops of the trees at the edge of the jungle. In a few minutes, the sun would be visible.

Not far from the car he saw a girl, in a yellow dress, face down in the grass. He dashed to her, knelt and recognized it was Laura Sanchez. "Laura. It's Lou DeRosa." He turned her over and lurched back at the sight of blood on her clothes and hands. Chills ran through his body and his heart raced. The possibility of nearby danger flashed into his mind. Out of the corner of his eye, he noticed someone lying on their back at the edge of the jungle. He glanced at Laura and then to the other person. She was his concern now even though there were no visible signs of wounds on her body. He wiped blood and grass from her face and tapped her cheek.

Laura blinked, sucked in a deep breath and her eyes popped open.

"It's Mr. DeRosa, come on, get up."

She clung to his arm as he helped her to her feet. Laura leaned against him as they staggered to his pickup. She climbed into the passenger's seat, closed her eyes and let her head rest against the back window.

Lou's first thought was to get something wet to wipe her face. He saw the beer bottle on the dash and grabbed it. The words written across the label, 'JAX, Best Beer in Town', jumped out at him. He shook his head and tossed the bottle to the ground. Old reliable, the army canteen was his backup. He snatched it from the floorboard, poured water into his hand and wiped her forehead.

Laura's eyes fluttered open and panned across the interior of the truck.

"Can you hear me?" he asked.

She looked at him and blinked. "Yes."

"Good, listen."

Lou handed her the canteen. "Wait here. Don't leave the truck, I'll be right back."

He hastened to the body near the jungle and stopped, recoiling and clenching his teeth. Light-headedness came over him and his legs weakened. After a momentary pause, he knelt and steadied himself with both hands on the ground. Lou shivered at the sight of the wounds. "Jesus, Mary and Joseph... Ed Robinson."

Lou sprang to his feet, brushed dirt and blood from his knees and wiped his bloody hands on his pants.

Leaves rustled inside the jungle and he turned toward the sound. *Leaves and branches do not move on their own.* The possibilities of what might have made the noise flashed through his mind. He backed away from the vegetation, spun around and scrambled to his pickup.

His blood stained hand trembled as he touched Laura's pale face. "You Okay?"

"Yes, why?"

"What did that to Ed?"

Laura's eyes narrowed and her head tilted. "Ed? When?"

Lou raced to the driver's side of the pickup and jumped behind the wheel. He fumbled to start the engine and fishtailed onto the dirt road.

Chapter IV

A 400 YEAR-OLD WOMAN

Dan's unmarked Chevy Biscayne occupied the supervisor's parking space near the door to the Gatun Locks Engineering Section. He and Lou stood near the trunk. Juan Escobar, the night shift team leader, stood with them. The three men turned and watched the Coroner's Office Parkway station wagon, and a tow truck pulling the Impala, pass by the building.

Dan looked at the concrete, furrowed his brow and thought of the last time Ed came to his house to pick up Carol. He collected himself. "Glad it wasn't her," he muttered.

"What ya say," Lou asked.

Dan's head snapped up, and he raised his eyebrows. "Glad Juan was here."

Juan stared at Lou's blood stained pants. His low voice quivered. "The girl wasn't in danger."

"What the hell you talkin about?" Lou asked.

"Women are never killed."

Dan looked at him and frowned. "Tell that to Jack the Ripper."

Juan shuffled his feet and tugged on his fingers. "People won't believe this."

"What?" Lou asked.

"You're talking crazy," Dan said.

Juan's wide eyes turned to Lou, and he took a deep breath. "You found a man killed by Tu Tu Vieja."

Dan raised his eyebrows. "Tu Tu what?"

"The Lady of the Lantern. The locals call her Tu Tu Vieja," Lou said.

Dan crossed his arms and his gaze bounced between the two men.

Lou pressed his lips together, turned to Juan and shrugged. "You think that old story is true?"

"It is. My grandmother saw her."

"Why ain't more people killed?" Lou asked.

"They have been."

Dan was not a newcomer to Panama. Over the years, he heard passing remarks of a female ghost that killed people, but he had not paid much attention to the story. He did not have the slightest clue why Lou and Juan were discussing more dead people, and Juan's grandmother seeing a lantern lady.

Lou smirked. "Yeah, dead guys are everywhere."

"The bodies disappear," Juan said. He made the sign of the cross. "Something made the old lady mad."

Dan mouth fell open, and he threw up his hands. "Wait a goddamn second. You trying to tell me an old lady did this?"

Lou nodded. "That's what he's saying, a four hundred-year-old lady."

"What?" Dan asked.

Lou shrugged. "It's old Panamanian folklore."

Dan sighed and shook his head. "Here we go again, another fucking Panamanian fairytale."

Juan, shocked by his comment, stared at him. "You won't find her Detective Casey, many people have tried."

Dan shoved a finger at him. "I'm not looking for a fuckin ghost. I'm gonna find a killer or kill a big ass cat." He stepped to his car door. "Come on, Lou."

They climbed into the car and Lou tapped the plastic leprechaun hanging from the rear-view mirror. "Where we headed?"

"Back up there. I need to check it out again." Dan turned the steering wheel toward Parker's Place.

"Ya know Ralph ain't goin to be happy," Lou said.

"About what?"

"Juan thinkin the Lady of the Lantern killed Ed. It won't take long for the locals to start talkin."

"So what's new?"

"He'll be pissed when he finds out."

"It's Ralph, that's the way he is."

Dan stopped on the grass adjacent a wall of dense jungle. He and Lou got out. "Wait here."

Lou cocked his head to the side. "Am I supposed to be scared?"

"Okay come on, keep your eyes open."

Lou rolled his eyes and followed Dan to the edge of the jungle. "Jesus, the blood, it's everywhere."

"He bled out."

Lou edged close to the dense foliage. He pointed at broken branches. "Look."

Dan leaned into the brush and spotted a large paw impression in the dirt. A circular indention, twelve inches behind the paw print, caught his eye. "Take a peek at this."

Lou shoved a plant aside and looked at the ground. "You're right. That's a big-ass cat."

"Any ideas why that round spot is behind it?" Dan asked.

Lou shrugged. "Nope."

Dan shook his head, and bit his lower lip. "A cat didn't make that mark in the ground."

They stepped from the jungle and Dan looked up at the sky. "If it's not a cat, how the hell do I start looking for a killer, when a bunch of irrational Panamanians are sure a spirit lady did it?"

Lou tapped him on the back. "Ya ain't got a chance in hell my friend, ya ain't got a chance."

Chapter V

FOLKLORE

Dan and Alisa, both exhausted, relaxed on the couch. Carol, their lanky sixteen-year-old daughter, shuffled toward the hallway.

"You okay darling?" Dan asked.

"Yeah, Dad." She continued down the hall.

He turned to his wife. "How is she doing?"

"Not great, she's been crying whenever someone calls."

Dan got up and started toward the hallway.

"Wait till later, Dan. She needs time alone."

"She might not talk to me, but tell her I'll listen if she wants to discuss it."

Alisa nodded. "How's the investigation going?" She tapped the couch.

"So far it makes as much sense as surgery to create a new belly button." He sat beside her. "Kind of crazy, but one of your compadres from Colon told me an old lady with claws killed him."

Alisa's eyelids rose, she twisted her wedding ring and diamond around her finger. "Tu Tu Vieja?"

"That's what the guy up at the locks called her. Lou said she was the Lady of the Lantern."

"It's a folk tale, passed from generation to generation by the local Panamanians."

Dan's gaze lingered on her. What he saw was the same girl he had met during their days together at Boston College. In his eyes, she remained the young woman full of her mother's stories of intrigue, and tales of danger in the jungle. He smiled. "Look babe. An old witch didn't kill that kid."

Alisa focused on him. "She's not a witch, people believe it."

Dan took a breath and shook his head. "It's just another fabricated tale to scare kids. If it's not a story of how chicken feet dust keeps monsters away, it's the slime off a snail's ass curing jock itch."

Alisa slapped him on the arm. "It isn't like that. The story goes back to when the Spanish first came to Panama. Soldiers traveled along the banks of the Chagres River.

When they came to a village, they raped and killed a local woman's daughter. She tried to stop them but they were too powerful."

"Was it near Gatun Lake?"

Alisa glanced up and rolled her eyes. "It was four hundred years ago. The lake formed when they built the Canal."

Dan nodded and attempted to shake his head at the same time. "I know that. What happened next?"

"The Spaniards cut off the mother's hands and feet, they sewed on jaguar paws."

"Hands and feet?"

Alisa nodded. "Yeah. Now she roams the lake and jungle and takes out her revenge on evil men."

Dan paused and stared at his wife. "She's got jaguar paws?"

"I told you that."

"Okay babe. Let me make sure I have this correct. Four hundred years ago, musket ball soldiers, cut the hands and feet off a woman. They then pull out their handy surgical kit and sew the severed paws of a large jungle cat on the ends of her arms and legs? Did these conquistadors have other magical powers?"

Alisa's fixed her eyes on him. He knew, at any moment, they would burn a hole through his forehead.

"I love you Dan, but sometimes you're an asshole. The story is folklore, will you please listen?"

Dan hugged her. "Babe, I love you and your mother very much, but I don't believe in spirits, phantoms or ghosts that troop around the jungle at night."

Alisa pressed her lips together. "Is that right?" She shoved a finger toward the leprechaun figurine on the small table. "You want to explain the scary little shoemaker over there. O'Grady, your family even gave him a name."

Dan stared at leprechaun figurine. He could not forget the first night, at age six, when the little man appeared in his dreams. His mother spent the next few weeks telling him stories of Ireland and the little magical shoemakers who hid their pots of gold in the countryside. A month later, he saw the figurine in a store and asked her to buy it for him. "He's been around since I was a kid. Father MacGillivray said he's here to cause mischief."

She grabbed his arm. "See, even the priest believes he's real."

"Yeah, but the priest never said O'Grady runs around killing people."

"Do you love me Dan?"

"Gimme me a break, of course I do."

Alisa slid beside him and took his hand. "I want nothing to happen to you. I've got a bad feeling, please listen."

"Okay."

"There's a woman who can tell you everything you need to know about Tu Tu Vieja."

"Who is she?"

"They call her Tierra. She lives in Old Town Colon."

"Where?"

"I'm not sure."

"How did you hear about her?"

"Colon's small, no one remains unknown. You must convince her it wasn't Tu Tu Vieja."

"Why?"

"The story of the Lady of the Lantern is too important to the women of Panama."

Chapter VI

THE BOSS

The next morning Dan could not shake what Juan and Lou said from his mind. If the locals thought a spirit woman killed Ed, and the people in the Canal Zone went along with them, he wouldn't get much support. *Maybe a cat did it, but not a ghost.*

Dan slipped into the Captain's office and felt the cool breeze from the small air conditioner hanging in a window. "Busy Ralph?"

Captain Ralph Phillips, born and raised in the Canal Zone, rarely took time for himself. Dan wondered how a man in his early fifties could think of nothing except work. For the past twelve years, he had been the Cristobal District Police Commander. An inch thick pile of paperwork lay on the large wooden desk in front of the big man.

Dan glanced at the framed photo on the corner of the desk. Young Ralph stood with his parents outside their home. His mother wore a white Pollera, the traditional embroidered Panamanian dress.

Ralph turned the top page over and shuffled the stack aside. "I'm always busy. What is it... anything new with the investigation?"

"It may take longer than I thought."

"Christ Dan. It looks open and closed to me. Just finish it."

Dan paused. "I need to make sure I don't overlook anything important."

Ralph shook his head and sighed. "A kid who should have known better, walks to the edge of the jungle at night. A big puma rips his throat open. What's so damn difficult?"

Dan had been through Ralph's probing questions many times. His anger grew, but he calmed himself. Both men tolerated each other to a point of friendship. Ralph knew Dan was the best criminal investigator in the Canal Zone and had no wish to become the next commander. Their relationship was a two-layer cake of conflict covered with mutual respect icing.

"I wish it was that easy. I need more time to check on a few things."

"Okay. What kinds of things need clarifying?"

"Was it a cat that killed him?"

"You saw the kid. What the hell else can make those wounds?"

"The Lady of the Lantern."

Ralph pressed his lips into a grim line.

Dan had seen the same serious look, each time Ralph said people born outside the Canal Zone didn't understand.

"Tu Tu Vieja. You sure you want to get into that?"

Dan shrugged and nodded. "Yeah. I have to, it'll help close the case."

"You'll find it will cause problems with the locals."

"Tough."

"They'll raise hell."

"They'll get over it."

"Don't piss them off, Dan."

"I'll try. If we're lucky, they won't put dried chicken blood or goat shit on our front steps."

Chapter VII

OLLIE'S PLACE

Lou sat on his regular bar stool at the Knights of Columbus and spun a half empty bottle of Jax beer between two fingers. Ceiling fans pushed hot air around a large room surrounded by louvered windows. A hardwood bar took up one wall and tables and chairs were evenly spaced across the floor.

Ollie, a bald, heavyset man with a thick neck, stood behind the bar. He looked Asian, but no one had any idea where he started his life. He had been the bartender for longer than anyone remembered. Lou recalled hearing people say he was Chinese. Others said he came from Mongolia as if they could point to the place on a globe. Ollie always kept a watchful eye on his customers, especially the teenagers who frequented the KC for hamburgers.

Lou glanced at the framed captioned photo of a large reptile hanging on the wall above the liquor bottles. He read the words under the picture. "Giant Gatun Lake Crocodile." Whenever someone new came into the bar and saw the picture, they would claim they saw one larger than the monster in the photo. *Bullshit always starts with the words 'Once upon a time'.*

Dan walked to the bar and sat on the stool next to him.

"Jesus Lou. Why do you drink that cheap shit?"

"It's good beer and ice cold. Ollie charges me ten cents a bottle."

Dan shoved a finger in the air and dropped two dollar bills on the bar. "Ollie, one ice cold beer and black rum with a splash of coke."

"Jax?" Ollie asked.

"No, Pab."

Ollie leaned over the cooler. Liquor bottles packed the counter behind him. In front of the bottles a meat cleaver stood upright, its tip embedded in the wood. It was well within Ollie's reach.

"How's Carol takin it?" Lou asked.

"It's been tough on her. She lost a good friend."

"Ralph still got you doin the investigation?"

"Yeah."

"Is he on your ass?"

"Nothing will change. He's been on it for twelve years."

"You're a kid from Boston. To him, you'll always be an outsider."

"I'm still working. I must do something right." Dan watched his fingernails tap against the bar. "Remember that lantern lady Juan mentioned?"

"Tu Tu Vieja," Lou said.

"Who told you the story?"

"A few guys I worked with many years ago when I first came here."

"You believe it?"

Ollie slid a Pabst Blue Ribbon bottle in front of Lou and placed a rum and coke in front of Dan. He scooped up one dollar.

Lou shoved the Jax bottle aside. "Ya kiddin me, hell no. Both of us know it would have taken a big cat to rip apart the kid's neck and do that much damage to his body. I don't expect you'll find a large jaguar stupid enough to be seven hundred miles north of its home turf."

Both men took a long drink.

"You sure?"

Lou turned to him and nodded. "I came here over fifty years ago. I've walked through this jungle, day and night."

"Ever see a jungle cat?"

"Sure, ocelots and jaguarondi." Lou pointed at the photo. "Big ass crocodile chased me, snakes scared the shit out of me, but I can't say I've seen a big puma or jaguar. And, I ain't seen an old lady with claws."

Ollie slid four hamburgers on the bar near Dan. "Four hamburga, you pay now," he yelled.

A skinny teenager stepped to the bar and dropped two quarters beside the plates.

Ollie slapped a hand on the bar, reached back and clamped his fingers around the cleaver handle. "Four hamburga, you pay two."

Dan nodded to Ollie and turned to the kid. "You owe him another fifty cents."

The kid rolled his eyes at Dan, dropped another two quarters on the bar and took the plates.

Dan grabbed the young man's shirtsleeve. "I'll bet you won't have that smirk on your face when I tell your father you tried to steal food from the KC."

"Sorry Mr. Casey," the kid replied and shuffled away.

Lou tilted his head toward Ollie. "Glad he's harmless."

"They shouldn't try to take advantage of him."

"What were you sayin?" Lou asked.

"Ralph believes I'll have a hard time with the locals."

"Well, the story is passed from one generation to the next. To them, she's real."

Dan finished his drink. He got up, tapped Lou on the shoulder and pointed at the cleaver. "Don't piss off Ollie."

Lou looked at him and smiled. "Me? I sharpen it for him. He wants to keep everyone honest."

"You're right. Do me a favor."

"What?" Lou asked.

"For now, don't go fishing up at the locks."

Lou laughed. "Why? Ya think cat lady might come after an unarmed old man?"

"No, but a killer may."

Chapter VIII

PACO AND SANCHA

Dan glanced at his watch and wiped his forehead. *Near midnight and the humidity is still ninety-nine percent.*

He weaved through a throng of people navigating the crowded main street in downtown Colon. Litter lined the gutters in front of seedy bars. Salsa and Soca music flowed from smoke filled doorways. Sweat soaked bodies trudged up the packed, uneven, sidewalk. He focused on the faces of people: the rich, the poor, drunks, workers, johns, whores and even a few who were sober. Downtown Colon was not his favorite place to visit, but locals working in the Canal Zone loved to talk and the important happenings of the day spread from person to person along its streets. Dan needed information and his contacts in and around the bars were his best sources.

He smiled when he saw Paco, the Panamanian Night Urchin, milling around on a nearby corner. The small time thief earned extra money for his family as Dan's informant. Screwing with him was something Dan loved to do because Pace was afraid of two things, jail and his own shadow. He approached the short dark man from the back. *Let's see if I can scare the shit out of him.*

"Paco," he said in a deep whisper.

Paco spun toward him. His hand grabbed at his heart and spittle dropped on the front of his shirt. After collecting himself, he wiped his shirt and smiled, exposing gaps between rotted teeth.

"What the po-leese need this midnight?"

"Information," Dan replied.

"The teef robe the gringo?"

"No. I need to find an old lady."

Paco grinned and spit in the gutter. "The old oors stay in the bars man."

"Not whores, a woman who lives in Old Town."

"Her have a name?"

"People call her Tierra," Dan said.

Paco froze, his face turned ashen as he lowered his voice and glanced at people passing nearby. "Why ya lookin for the bad time?"

"The boy at Gatun, you know about it?" Dan asked.

"All da people hear the story."

"So, how do I find the bad time lady?"

"Better you not."

Paco enjoyed playing hard to get, but the little man's weakness was his mother. Dan flashed a five-dollar bill. "Did your mother enjoy the food you bought her after the last time we talked?"

"Her do, Mista Dan. Her love you and the money in ya pocket."

"So let's talk, but if you can't tell me how to find Tierra I'll ask someone else." He smirked and returned the five to his pocket.

"Wait, you too jipsy man."

Paco glanced side to side and leaned in close. Dan tilted away.

"Ya know Sancha, she a red skin thing?"

"Yeah, everyone says she's pretty."

"Her at the Fanta-see. The obeah woman is she friend."

Dan handed him the money. "Thanks. Tell your mother I was asking for her and wish her good health."

Paco smiled and shoved the money in his pocket. "Her love you more tonight, Mista Dan."

Dan grinned, slid a dollar from his pocket and held it out to Paco. "Here, get a sweet pastry and tell her I bought it for her."

He ambled up the street and heard Paco behind him.

"Dat old woman, her scar-ry. Look wit two eyes and watch the back-side."

Dan stepped into the doorway of the Fantasy Bar and smiled. It was not the Ritz, but the tourist with money to blow and Navy Chiefs, described it as classy compared to most of the dives on the strip. Tonight a crowd packed the joint.

He lingered at the entrance. Ceiling fans launched smoke around somewhat higher-class patrons and prettier whores. Girls hung on men who staked out their treasured spots at the bar. A jukebox belted out Soca music and lights flashed. On the dance floor, two girls, their olive skin glistening with perspiration, ground their hips to the beat.

Dan fixed his eyes on Sancha, a young curvaceous Caribbean doll and a first year college educated tease. Besides being the assistant manager and his friend, she was a wealth of information on the daily happenings in Colon. She kept up with the gossip in town and people loved to tell her everything legal, and illegal, happening on the streets.

Sancha spotted him, extended her arms and batted her eyes. She kissed his cheek and pulled him to a corner table.

"Out late tonight," she said, with a suggestive wink.

"I need help."

"Anything for my favorite policeman." She dragged two chairs from the empty table and shoved them together. Their hips touched when they sat next to each other.

"It's about the dead boy."

"At Gatun?" Her arm glided behind his chair and a mischievous finger drew patterns on his back.

"Yeah."

"What can I do?"

Dan raised his eyebrows. "There are crazy stories flying around the Canal Zone."

She frowned and tilted her head. "I don't understand."

"Claws ripped the kid apart."

Sancha stiffened and her finger stopped making designs on his back. She withdrew her arm from behind him. "You saw the body?"

"It wasn't a pretty sight."

She squirmed in her chair. "People have been talking, but I didn't believe it."

"A local up at Gatun said an old lady killed him. One of my friends called her the Lady of the Lantern."

Sancha took in a deep breath, glanced into his eyes and looked away. Her voice shook. "People call her Tu Tu Vieja."

"Lady of the Lantern, Tu Tu Vieja, whatever the hell they say."

Sancha glared at him and remained silent.

"Alisa thinks I need to learn more about this crazy story."

"The story is not crazy, and I know Alisa wouldn't tell you that."

"You're right, but she told me to talk with a woman in Old Town."

"Old Town?" Sancha pondered. "Who?"

"Her name is Tierra."

Her eyes widened, and she took a moment to adjust her blouse.

That was a surprise.

"Is she in trouble?"

"No."

"Why... Why do you want to talk with her?"

"A four hundred-year-old woman killed no one. I'd like to prove it."

"You believe Tierra can help?"

Dan paused and stared at her. Sancha's expression told him she was uncomfortable answering questions "Yeah if she will educate a gringo cop." His friend and informant was protecting the old woman. *Maybe extra pressure will help.* "Someone told me you know her, you and her are friends." Dan saw a slight nod.

She glanced around and lowered her voice. "You need to understand many people are afraid to speak of Tu Tu Vieja. Tierra may not want to talk to you."

"It's important, Sancha. I need to meet her."

Sancha pushed her chair away from the table. "I'll be back in a minute." She headed across the room to an interior door.

Dan stared at the door when it closed. It was odd she had been apprehensive to talk about Tierra. The woman was important to her.

His eyes drifted around the room. In a dim corner, a bald three hundred and fifty pound man, dressed in black, sat behind a table. Shadows and his dark skin hid his six foot seven inch frame. They were not friends but shared a bond of mutual respect. One night, months ago, a man sitting next to Dan tried to pocket ten dollars of his money. With a simple squeeze, the bouncer crushed the bones in the thief's hand. The jerk pulled a knife on the big guy but set it on the bar when Dan shoved his pistol against his ribs. Two strong rums and a few choice words later, his new acquaintance walked back to his secluded corner.

The bartender strolled up and placed a drink in front of him. "Black rum, tip of coke."

"That's it," Dan replied. He reached into his pocket.

"On the ouse," the bartender said.

Wonder what he thinks? "Thanks. You believe in the Lady of the Lantern?"

The bartender stared at him. "Vieja?"

Dan nodded. "Yeah."

The bartender shrugged. "Woman believe. Man skear'd."

"You scared?"

He broke eye contact with Dan, forced a laugh and plodded away.

Dan sipped his drink, his eyes darting between the girls and their patrons. If someone yelled 'Tu Tu Vieja' loud enough, he figured most of the people in the bar would piss their pants.

He looked across the room when he saw Sancha come out the door. She edged up to the table and slipped into the chair opposite him. "She'll meet with you." Inching a note from her bra, she slid it across the table. "It's down an ally in Old Town, not far from here. The door has a sun and moon painted on it." She placed a hand on his arm. "Be careful. Old Colon can be dangerous."

"O'Grady will keep me safe."

"Do you believe he can?"

"Hasn't failed me yet." Dan stood and removed a few crisp bills from his pocket. He extended a, let's dance hand, to her.

She took it, squeezed and stood.

"Thank you," he said. He stuffed the bills between her breasts.

"Come back when you have more time," she teased.

Chapter IX

OLD TOWN COLON

Dan turned onto a narrow alley, still damp from an earlier rain. An occasional uncovered light bulb, above a door, lit the gray paving stones and concrete walls. *Never been here.* Nothing moved except a man and a woman in the shadows groping each other. He scanned the note and stepped to the center, passing the well-occupied couple. *Way too busy to pay attention.*

Partway up the street, a man turned from the darkness of a doorway and strolled towards him. The closer he came, the more the hair stood up on Dan's arms.

The man took the center of the pavement and challenged Dan's path.

Dan locked his eyes on dirty pants and a grimy white shirt. He quit walking and sighed. Rats scurried past his feet and dove under a pile of garbage.

"You a saila man?"

Dan lowered his head and looked at his own shoes and pants. He focused on the man and smiled. "Do I look like a fucking sailor?"

The guy flashed a broad grin.

Another major challenge for the local dentist.

"Ya think ya ass is bad?"

"No, but my wife says I'm an asshole."

The man shuffled within arm's reach, sized Dan up, and exposed a hunting knife attached to his tattered belt.

It took less than a second for the man's foul breath and sour smelling clothing to reach his nose. *If I hit him, I bet crawling critters will leap out of his pockets.* Dealing with the lower end of the food chain did not annoy him, but he had his limits. The guy had to be a thief, and he didn't want to take his eyes off him. Dan stared at the man as he turned his head, sucked in air, and held his breath.

"Ya ave money?"

Dan nodded and raised his eyebrows. "I sure do, but it's not enough for my expensive rum and your cheap whore."

"Gimme money or I going tek it." He flashed a grim smile.

The years Dan spent working the streets taught him to make the first move. The man who waits to react, surrenders his advantage. "We were discussing my rum and your whore," Dan said, as his right hand swept to his back. He pulled a 45 automatic from his waistband and thrust the cold heavy muzzle under the would-be robber's chin. It took little pressure to bury the tip of the barrel a quarter inch in soft tissue. His thumb pulled back the hammer.

The robber's eyes widened and beads of sweat formed on his forehead.

Dan addressed his victim in the soft somber tone of a parish priest. "Tonight my friend, you are an unlucky man." He ground the muzzle into loose skin. "You must have flunked robbery class in school because you didn't learn shit."

With eyes focused down his nose, the man trembled.

Dan's stomach burned and his throat filled with acid. He could not keep taking small gulps of air, hold his breath and stay alert. Avoiding the smell was not a good reason to give the guy an opening. With two fingers, he lifted the knife from the man's belt and slung it into the trash heap. Rats scrambled from the rubbish and Dan wiped his fingers on his pants. He wet his lips and continued to preach. "Only a dumb ass would rob the man about to send him to meet Jesus."

From his left pocket, Dan removed a six-inch switchblade. His thumb pressed the small button and a gleaming razor sharp blade sprang out. "After I kill you, I will slice you up and the police will believe Tu Tu Vieja stopped by for a little practice on a lost soul sneaking around the back alleys of town."

The thief sobbed.

Dan shoved the man away and leveled the pistol on his forehead. "Tonight Jesus will not be happy when he sees your ugly ass show up at the pearly white gates."

Large eyes focused on the muzzle of Dan's pistol. The thief raised his hands as if he was praying. "Please."

Dan lowered the pistol to the man's chest and his voice softened. "A miracle, your luck changed. Your only sin is mopery with intent to creep. Quick, run!"

The robber spun around, flung his upper body forward and fell.

Dan took a step and kicked him in the ass to get him on his way. He sucked in a deep breath of stale air, lowered the hammer and slid the 45 into his back waistband.

The street in front of him was empty. After a two-minute walk, he spotted a door with a sun and moon painted on weathered wood. The door swung open before he came within ten feet of it.

A boy stood in the doorway and motioned him into the house. "Her way-tin in back."

Dan bent his six foot two inch frame to enter the tiny dim room. It took a second to scan his surroundings. The sparse furnishings were a couch, two wooden chairs and a small round table in a shadow against the wall. The boy pointed to a doorway covered by bright plastic beads strung on monofilament line held down with used lead fishing weights. Candle light flickered from inside the room. Parting the beads, he entered.

Tierra, a silver-haired woman with a timeworn face, sat hunched over a round table. Two short candles stood in a plate covered with wax. A blood red scarf provided contrast to her white dress.

Dan peered into the dark shadows around the room. The first thing he noticed was a ten-inch long black jaguar paw hanging on the wall. Five large pearl colored claws extended from the black fur. He raised a hand, looked at his fingers, and then back at the claws. *They're as big as my fingers.* In a corner of the room, a red cloth lay across a large stone bowl atop a six-inch high wooden table. Dark stains marked the tabletop. *Blood on an altar if that's what you call it.*

Tierra motioned to a chair opposite her. "Please sit," she said, with a slight English accent.

Dan paused, took a second look at the paw, and sat. He stopped breathing the instant he looked into Tierra's eyes. The old woman's young eyes sparkled as none he had ever seen. The white of her eyes was as unblemished as new fallen snow. Each pupil and iris were one, black as a starless sky. She did not blink or move her eyes from his, during the time he stared at her. He took a breath.

"I need your help."

"I know why you have come."

"Did Sancha tell you?"

She ignored his question. "You seek the oldest jaguar."

"Not a jaguar, a killer." Dan looked at the jaguar paw and kept talking. "People told me the story of the Spaniards and the old woman."

Tierra studied him a moment. "So your ears work well, but I know and see the people she killed and the men never found."

"Maybe so, but an old woman didn't kill that boy." Dan noticed her eyes open wider when he said the word boy. *Let it pass... let's see where it goes.*

Tierra tilted her head to the side. "She is not a woman. She is not a jaguar. The lady is a creation of man, not of God."

"I don't think so," he said.

"Do you know men suffer her revenge?"

Dan nodded. "The story is nothing more than folklore believed by superstitious people."

"You are correct, Detective Casey. What you forgot to consider is superstitious people often trust their beliefs and most men fear them. They hear and see things they cannot understand." She closed her eyes and lowered her head. She whispered. "Your lady is fine but I see a dark spirit near Carol and a cloud of danger behind you."

Dan's muscles stiffened and his comfort level dropped. "How do you know my daughter's name?"

Tierra opened her eyes and stared into his. "I see and know many things, much more than you."

"Is she in danger?" he asked.

"For now she is safe, but she stands near a jaguar that will kill again."

Dan's eyes locked on the old woman. "Tu Tu Vieja?"

A smile came to her lips. "You told me her name."

"Yeah, but that doesn't mean I believe she's real."

"What you believe is not important. What has happened and what will happen is."

"Is my family in danger?"

Tierra looked into his eyes and raised a finger. "One will pay."

Dan frowned. "What do you mean?"

"You said people told you the story. If you listened, what I said should not be difficult for you to understand."

Dan had enough. He was not prepared to question the woman. She spoke in riddles, and he could not figure out if what she said was a threat or a warning. He stood, dropped two dollar bills on the table and pointed at the paw hanging on the wall. "Why do you have that on your wall?"

"The hand protects this house. Evil men will not come here."

He furrowed his brow and turned to leave. "Thank you."

On his way to the bead-covered door, he heard her say, "We shall speak again, Detective Casey."

Chapter X

THE OLD MAN

An old man sat in a hollowed out log kayak cut from a single tree trunk. The locals called it a cayuco.

He drifted on dark placid water, two hundred yards from the entrance to the Gatun Locks. With his fishing pole over the water, he watched a Panama Canal Pilot boat turn in his direction. The closer the large boat came, the more alarming the wake forming behind it looked. The swell rolled toward his tiny craft. He dropped the fishing pole into the boat and grabbed the paddle. *That wave knock me wrong side, me swimming tonight.* A man bobbing in the water in the middle of the night was like ringing a dinner bell to the nearest large crocodile. He shuddered at the prospect of becoming a meal for a large reptile as he turned his boat into the wave. The small craft rose four feet and slid down the back side of the swell. A second smaller wave followed, thankfully, it preceded calm water. As he dug his paddle deep into the water, the cayuco turned toward the fading Pilot boat. He shoved his middle finger into the air. "Damn cowboys!"

The old man reeled in his line, started paddling toward shore and saw the flicker of a lantern light on the water. *Someone fishin.* He lifted his paddle, watched the light glide to shore and go out. At night, few anglers were on the lake. He lowered his paddle and continued toward land.

A small boat protruding from the mangroves came into view. He looked at the narrow craft and furrowed his forehead. *Dat cayuco is old, green moss cover da side.* Setting his paddle between his legs, he raised both hands to his mouth. "Hello, who is here?" No response came. "You too highfalutin to talk?" he yelled. He grabbed the paddle and headed toward a spot near the empty cayuco. The bow of his boat pushed into a dark wall of vegetation and slid onto solid ground. He scooted to the front and eyed the black expanse. "Anyone here?" he said. He stood and planted one foot on the ground.

A black paw exploded from the bush, tearing flesh from his scalp and face.

###

Juan sat at his desk reading the local Spanish language newspaper. Since the night Ed died, he and every other person working at the locks remained on edge. The night shift provided him with one safety advantage, he turned the deadbolt on the door the moment he entered his office. A telephone ring shattered the silence. He jumped in his seat, shook his head and slapped the paper shut. *What now.*

"Engineering, Juan," he said into the handset. His teeth clenched, and he glanced at the wall clock. "I get off in fifteen minutes." He shoved the newspaper aside and pushed away from the desk. "I'm on my way." *The sun's up, I should be goin home.*

When he stepped from the door of a building alongside the canal, he saw Hector waving his arms at the edge of the lock. "Hurry!"

Juan trotted to him. "What's wrong?"

Hector raised his hands, "Everything." He turned and headed for the lock gate at the entrance to the Lake. Juan increased his pace to keep up with him.

A hundred yards from the entrance to the lock, a stationary container ship waited. A small cayuco bobbed in the water near the ship's bow. Juan's mouth fell open when he saw a leg hanging over the side of the small craft.

"All operation into the locks is shut down," Hector said.

He and Hector reached the front of the lock. Both men grabbed emergency lifejackets from a pole and scurried down a ladder. They reached a rowboat tied to a rung in front of the gate. Juan slid to the bow while Hector plopped on the bench seat and grabbed the oars. He lowered them into the water and heaved the boat into motion.

"The pilot has been raising hell. Lake traffic will back up because that drunken asshole passed out," Hector said.

Juan glanced over his shoulder at the leg hanging over the side of the wooden boat. "I hope he's drunk and had no heart attack." He turned toward the bow, held on to the gunwale, and looked back at Hector. Sweat rolled down the back of Hector's neck as he dug the oars into the water. Juan watched him for a moment. Both men were oblivious to the direction or speed of the rowboat.

Juan turned back toward the bow. His body tensed and hands clamped onto the sides of the boat. "Slow down!"

The rowboat slammed into the side of the log dugout. The collision propelled Juan forward. His head stopped inches above the slashed and blood dried face of an old man. "Holy Jesus!" he screamed, squeezing his eyes shut. Gasping to fill his lungs, he fought his way back into the rowboat. His mouth filled with an acid taste, and he vomited over the side.

Chapter XI

KING ERIC

A group of men gathered in the grass along the shore beside the locks. Juan, with his head buried in his arms, sat twenty feet away from them.

Eric Jankowski spotted Manuel Cabrera, a Canal Zone police officer, standing at the edge of the water. He walked up behind him. "Excuse me."

"Yeah," Manuel replied, without turning.

Eric cleared his throat to make sure he had Manuel's attention. *This is more important than your mindless police work.* "I am Eric Jankowski, the Gatun Locks Manager of Operations."

"Great, I'm busy at the moment," Manuel said, his eyes on Hector and the rowboat heading toward shore.

Eric did not appreciate lower level workers ignoring him. He let out an audible sigh and pointed at a ship. "That ship over there. It's waiting to enter the locks. All this is slowing down world commerce. We need to get it moving, now."

Manuel ignored him. "Good job Hector, keep coming this way."

Eric's face reddened, he shuffled his feet and raised his voice. "The ship needs to be lowered to the Atlantic."

"Not my problem. I can't help you with it."

"I know that damn it, you're just a cop," Eric hissed.

Manuel glanced over his shoulder. "I'm busy doing cop work, buddy." He pointed toward the grass. "Why don't you ask Juan, and be nice, he's the guy in charge out here."

Eric spun around and looked at an unmarked Chevy Biscayne pull up and park. Dan and Ralph got out and headed toward Manuel.

Now I will get a damn answer. Eric walked toward them and passed Juan. *Look at this peasant.* "Get off your ass and tell them to get that ship into the lock," he yelled.

Ralph waved. "Hi Eric, I'd say good morning, but it doesn't appear to be one."

"We need something done about this, Ralph. We can't have dead bodies shutting down traffic to the Atlantic."

"I agree Eric, we're working on it."

A simple agreement did not correct the problem. Eric shook a finger at him. "First was the kid, now it's someone else."

"Detective Casey is working the case. He's my best man, he'll figure it out."

Eric tensed and ground his teeth. "I want it stopped now or heads will roll."

"I'll pass your demand on to Tu Tu Vieja," Ralph said.

Eric glared at both men. *Cops have poor listening skills.* He stepped into Dan's personal space and shoved a finger at his chest. "Listen Casey. I want this whole mess..."

Dan took a half step forward and pressed his chest against Eric. "Mr. Jankowski. I suggest you shove that finger somewhere I can't see it. You have five seconds. If you don't, I'm going to bite it off and spit it back at you."

Ralph tapped Dan's arm and motioned for him to follow. They walked to Manuel.

###

Lou did not plan to fish, but he did want to see if those at the spillway were having any luck. When he approached the lake, he spotted the crowd and Dan's car. The old pickup stopped next to the Chevy Biscayne, and he waited for the truck to cough itself to death. He slid an open beer bottle onto the dash, climbed out and headed to Ralph.

"What did his highness of the Panama Canal Company say?" he asked Ralph.

"As if we don't have enough pressure, we get orders from his royal dumb ass."

"Orders?"

"Yeah, tell the killer to stop," Ralph said.

Lou shook his head. "Wow. And to think it took a four-year college degree to come up with that plan."

Hector threw a line to Manuel, who hauled the small boat and its lifeless cargo to shore. He glanced inside and turned away. "It's not nice."

Dan and Ralph looked at the body and Ralph turned his head.

"Has anyone called Doc Lopez?" Ralph asked.

"I told dispatch to call him. He's on his way," Manuel said.

Dan stared at the body and turned to Lou. "Why kill an old man?"

Chapter XII

THREE INCH CANINES

Dan walked into Ralph's office. His boss sat at his desk straightening a bent handcuff key.

"Where's Doc?" Dan asked.

"Talking to Manny... be here in a minute."

Doctor Paul Lopez, the part-time Coroner, trudged in with a folder under his arm. He pulled up a chair next to Dan, opened the folder and shuffled through a few pages.

"How's Carol?" Paul asked Dan.

"Not too bad. Alisa is keeping her busy."

During meetings in his office, Ralph liked to keep things official, but Dan seized upon an opportunity to find out what Doc was up to lately. "How's business with those who still have blood pressure?"

Paul shrugged. "Fishing hooks in arms, necks and heads, but during the last few days there's been a run on broken bones."

"No major wounds?" Dan asked.

"Small ones. Two kids in Cristobal hacked their way off of an imaginary Spanish galleon and got a little too close to each other."

Dan's eyebrows rose. "Nothing serious, I hope."

"No, only stitches. Thank God the machetes weren't sharp."

Ralph cleared his throat and waved a hand at Paul. "Okay, let's get back to work. Go ahead Paul."

Paul glanced at a page. "Didn't have time yet for the old man, but it looks as if we're in agreement. The wounds on Ed match those of a big cat."

"That's what I thought." Ralph smiled at Dan.

Paul tapped his notes. "Left paw struck his neck."

Dan thought the paw print he saw in the jungle after Ed died looked as if a large cat made it, but he had his doubts. The circular indention in the ground behind it kept popping back into his mind. "Those wounds were massive. How big a cat would it take to do that much damage?"

Paul nodded. "Bigger than any puma or jaguar we've seen around here. Don't think there's ever been a cat that size in Panama."

Dan scrunched his eyes and pursed his lips. "How much would this big cat weigh?"

Paul's forehead wrinkled. He tapped his pencil against the folder. "Three hundred plus pounds."

Dan raised his eyelids. "Wow. It would have big teeth, wouldn't it?"

Paul smiled and lifted a finger to show the size. "At least three inch canines."

"There were no bite marks," Dan said.

Paul shook his head. "No none."

Ralph's gaze bounced between the two men. "Lou drove up in that loud old clunker of his. The cat took off as soon as he arrived."

Dan tilted his head and stared at the wall for a moment. "What about the old man?"

"Haven't examined him, but from what I saw, large claws tore him apart."

"So we all agree. It was an unfortunate animal attack," Ralph said.

"One second." Dan turned to Paul. "Do me a favor."

"Sure, what?"

"Take a closer look at the kid's wounds and call me after you finish with the old man."

"Wrap it up and close it, Dan."

Dan was not about to give up that easy. He hoped Ralph would not take it personal. "You gave me the case, you want it back?"

Ralph glared at him.

Paul threw up his hands. "What the hell am I trying to find?"

"Can't answer that yet, maybe a killer." Dan slid his chair back and walked toward the door. He muttered loud enough for all to hear. "No bite marks, no cat."

XIII

WE WOULDN'T LIE

Steve, Jim and Warren sat in the grass near the edge of the lake at Parker's Place. Each held an open beer bottle and peered over gloomy moonlit water.

Steve tied a loose shoelace on one of his white tennis shoes. He turned his bottle over, shook it and watched two drops fall out. *Boring.* "We gonna sit here all night?"

Warren upended his empty bottle and hopped to his feet. "I'm done."

The boys trooped to Jim's rusted pickup truck. Jim lowered the tailgate and removed three beer bottles from a cooler and an opener from his pocket. They sat on the tailgate and shared the opener.

"We've been out here for an hour. I think that Tu Tu Vieja story is a bunch of crap," Jim said.

Steve glanced at Warren and raised his eyebrows. "You believe it?"

"I don't know. Everyone says you can see the lantern moving across the water, but none of them have ever seen it."

"Well, my mom believes it, and so does everyone in Colon," Steve said.

Warren swung his head toward the jungle twenty yards from the truck. "Ya hear that?"

"What?" Steve asked.

Warren pointed to the dense bush. "Something's over there."

Steve slid off the tailgate and trudged toward the dense overgrowth. He stopped, looked back at Jim and Warren, and smiled. "I'll see if it's the cat lady." He reached the edge of the foliage and yelled, "Chickens." Acting as if he was searching inside the thick vegetation, he parted branches and leaned into the bush. Leaves rustled, and a branch swayed. He jumped and shuffled backwards. A beam from car lights passed across him and the face of the jungle.

"Someone's coming," Jim yelled.

Steve ran to the pickup. Jim and Warren slid off the tailgate and looked down the dirt road.

"It's Carol's dad," Warren said.

"The cop, stash the beer," Jim said. He grabbed the cooler.

The awkward boys scrambled, shoving half-filled bottles in the cooler. Jim closed the tailgate.

Steve watched Dan's unmarked police car approach. *Wonder why he's here?*

Dan spotted the boys and shook his head. *What the hell are they doing up here this late. They need their heads examined.* He parked alongside Jim's pickup and stepped out.

"Hi Mr. Casey," Jim said.

Dan nodded and looked at Jim's truck. He spotted the cooler. "What are you lads doing?"

"We just got here," Steve said.

Dan caught a whiff of beer.

"From where, a brewery or a Colon strip joint? How old are you?"

"Seventeen, sir," Steve said.

Dan glanced at Steve's, dew-laden blood stained tennis shoes. He pointed toward the spot Ed died. "You been near the jungle where Ed died?"

"No sir," Warren said.

Dan chewed on his bottom lip and stared at Warren. Without taking his eyes off Warren, he raised his hand and pointed at Steve. "I asked him, not you."

"No, sir, we wouldn't lie," Steve said.

Dan drew in a deep breath and eased the air from his lungs. He pointed at Steve's shoes. "What's that bloody red shit on your shoes?"

Steve looked at the red dew clinging to his white shoes. He cringed and jumped in place, firmly scraping the soles and sides of each shoe on the grass. "I was there for a second."

Dan held up an arm. "Quit hopping around like an idiot. Who bought the beer?"

Steve stopped jumping but continued pressing his shoes into the grass.

"Both of them are old enough to buy beer in Colon," Jim said.

"Yeah, that's true, but you're in the Canal Zone not Colon." Dan walked to his car and opened the back door. "Put the cooler on the seat and hit the road."

The boys jostled to comply.

"All of you need to put your brains in gear. Something in that jungle killed your friend. Are you trying to become the next three victims?"

None of them said a word.

"Beat it. I don't want to see you up here again and tell your friends this place is off limits. Commander Phillips will want to talk with the parents of anyone caught in this area."

Dan watched the three boys scramble into Jim's pickup and drive toward the locks. *Harmless, but no brains. Better tell Ralph... this isn't a safe place to be at night.*

XIV

DIEGO

In a classroom on the second floor of Cristobal High School, Warren, Carol and Katy sat at student desks forming a half circle in the center of the room. Warren glanced at the open windows then turned and looked at Steve and three of his friends. They sat with their chairs backed up against the wall opposite the windows. Millie Walker, a forty-year-old teacher, occupied a large desk in front of the class. Behind her, in bold letters, 'Annual Talent Contest' covered half the blackboard.

The door opened and Diego, a six foot two inche muscular nineteen-year-old graduate, entered. A scar snaked its way from his forehead, across one eye and down his cheek. It stopped at his chin.

Warren watched Steve and his friends' chuckle at the sight of Diego. *One day Diego will kick their asses,* he thought.

Carol waved. "Diego." She motioned him to her group, and he dropped into a chair next to her.

"Where's Marie?" Carol asked.

"Out with friends from her class."

"She's going to LSU, isn't she?" Katy asked.

Diego nodded and smiled. "She started her junior year, majoring in anthropology."

"How old is she now?" Carol asked.

"In two months she'll be twenty-two."

Millie interrupted them. "Diego, come sit up here."

As Diego walked to the chair beside Mrs. Walker's desk, Warren heard Steve chuckle. He glanced at him. *Maybe tonight Steve, keep being a jerk.*

Diego had come close to death when a drunk merchant marine, in a truck, sideswiped his car and sent it off the road near Fort Gulick. He was lucky an army doctor saw the accident happen and stopped to help him.

Warren leaned to the girls. "I don't know why Diego wants to come back here." He tilted his head toward Steve and his friends. "They're being stupid and laughing at him because of his scar."

"Mrs. Walker told me she called him because she needed help with the contest," Katy said.

"After the accident, she visited him every day in the hospital. He'll never forget that and will do anything for her," Carol said.

"Those guys don't bother him, he told me they act like little kids," Katy added.

Warren whispered to Carol. "I need to talk to you."

"What is it?"

"Not here, later."

XV

CLAWS

Dan knocked twice on the doorframe and walked in to the Captain's office.

Ralph leaned back in his chair with one foot against the desk. Paul sat in one of two wooden chairs in front of it.

"Doc, Ralph." Dan nodded at both men and took a seat.

Ralph dropped his foot and scooted up to the desk. "Paul examined both bodies."

"Find anything?" asked Dan.

Paul grinned and raised a microscope slide of two black hairs pressed between pieces of glass. "I found the same hairs on both bodies."

Dan stared at the slide, squinted and nodded. "Jaguar hairs?"

"I don't know. It's hard to tell. They're coarse. I'd say animal, but I can tell you they're dyed black."

The two words 'dyed black' bounced around in Dan's brain. A smile crept across his face as he stared at the slide. "I'll be damned, dyed hair on a fake jaguar paw."

Paul's eyes widened, and he jumped out of his chair. "My wife has one!"

"One what?" Ralph asked.

Paul removed a key chain from his pocket. A small jaguar paw, the size of a black rabbit's foot with tiny pearl colored claws, hung from one end of the chain. "Drove her car today."

"Damn, I forgot about the key chains and even jewelry made into jaguar paws. They're all over Panama. Most women have a cat paw in their homes," Ralph said, leaning across his desk.

Dan glanced at the small paw dangling from the chain. "Does your wife believe that crazy lantern lady story?"

Ralph tapped his fingers on his desk. "It's Tu Tu Vieja, Dan."

"Come on boss, Tu Tu my ass. Both of you believe it, don't you?"

"That has nothing to do with the deaths of two people. I think we're all a little superstitious."

Over the years, Dan had listened to many stories of secret powers, ghostly figures and evil curses spoken at night. He did not give credence to them then, and he would not now. "I'm not," he said to Ralph

Ralph leaned back in his chair and folded his arms across his chest. "Sure you're not. Why don't you tell us the story of that leprechaun and your conversations with him?"

"He doesn't run around ripping people apart."

"You're from Boston," Ralph said.

"That's true, but I learn quickly." Dan pointed to the tiny jaguar paw in Paul's hand. "I've seen a paw a lot bigger than that one. It's ten times that size."

Ralph nodded his head. "Sure you did, where?"

"At an old lady's house in Colon."

"What old lady?"

"She's called Tierra."

Paul froze in his chair, his eyes bulged and he cleared his throat. "Ula," he whispered.

"What?" Ralph asked.

"Ula, that's her name. She practices Obeah."

Dan pursed his lips and scrunched his eyebrows. "That's the second time I heard the word Obeah. What the hell does it mean?"

"It's sorcery that started in West Africa and is like voodoo practiced in the Caribbean. I didn't know she was still alive," Paul said.

"And doing well," Dan added.

Paul stared at him a moment. "Few people in the Canal Zone know her."

"And you do?" asked Ralph.

Paul lowered his head. "My mother and she were friends."

Dan bit his lip to keep from grinning. He and Doc shared over ten years of friendship, but this was a complete surprise. It looked as if Doc's mother once had her own medical practice, but on a level a little closer to the local population.

"Did you see her?" Paul asked.

"Yes, we met the other day."

Paul exhaled and shook his head. "Ula's not a 'let's meet and talk' person."

Dan smiled. He slid his chair back.

"Where are you going?" Ralph asked.

"To see if she's available tonight. Want me to tell her you said hello, Paul?"

"Don't mention my name. Pissing her off once was enough."

Ralph frowned. "What did you do to her?"

"It's a long story."

Dan headed to the door and glanced back. "Keep digging, Captain, I'll bet it's a good one."

XVI

SOMEONE SAID SOMETHING

Alisa curled on the couch reading a book. She glanced up when Carol wandered in and began to meander around the room.

"Where's Dad?"

"He'll be home soon."

For the next few minutes, Carol continued back and forth across the floor and suddenly stopped. "My friends were talking about what happened to Ed."

"So is every other person in Panama," Alisa said, returning her eyes to the book.

"You know, Mom, maybe someone wanted to kill people."

Alisa looked at her. "That's crazy."

"Maybe not, maybe they had a reason."

"What reason could anyone have to kill another person?"

"Maybe people talk about him and laugh at him."

Alisa tilted her head and stared at her daughter. "Talk and laughter are not reasons to commit murder."

"Maybe... Maybe it really bothers him."

Alisa vaulted to her feet and slammed the book closed. "OK, enough maybe this and maybe that. What's bothering you?"

"Someone said something. I don't know if I should tell Dad."

"What?"

"One of the kids said he wanted to kill people."

Alisa jerked her head back and dropped the book. A sudden coldness raced across her chest, the pitch of her voice rose. "I'm calling..." She heard a car door slam and footsteps coming up the stairs.

Dan stepped in and kissed her on the cheek. "Hi, babe."

Alisa pointed at him. "You need to talk to your daughter."

He kissed Carol and took her hand.

Her husband would take his time as he always did when speaking to Carol. Calm conversations about murder, especially one committed by Tu Tu Vieja, did not exist in her world; too much Latin blood flowed through her veins. *How does he do it?*

He pulled Carol to the couch and Alisa stood over them.

"What can I do for my beautiful daughter?"

"Remember the boy who was in the car accident last year?"

"Which one, there must have been ten of them?"

"He has a long scar on his face."

"Yeah, Diego."

"His sister is Marie, right?" Alisa asked.

"Yeah, the real skinny girl," Carol said.

"What about him?" her father asked.

"The boys at school tease him."

"Didn't he graduate last year?" Dan asked.

Carol nodded. "Yeah, but Mrs. Walker called him and asked if he would help with the talent contest."

Dan pursed his lips. "So what do you mean, they tease him?"

"They call him Crash, and say he left part of his face on the steering wheel."

"How can they be so cruel? Why do they treat their..." Alisa stopped when she saw Dan looking at her with his head tilted to the side. "Sorry, go ahead, Carol."

"It really makes Diego mad when they do that."

Dan raised his eyebrows. "Please get to the point, darling."

"Diego's girlfriend said something."

Alisa could not stay still and kept shifting her weight from foot to foot. "Did she talk to you?" she asked.

"No, Mom, to Warren." Carol began to ramble at break-neck speed. "Warren and I both know her. She used to be Diego's girlfriend but they're not boyfriend and girlfriend now. She's friends with Warren... not his girlfriend. He told me, she told him that Diego told her he..."

Dan raised his hand in front of Carol. He gave her a quick hug and glanced at the leprechaun figurine on the table across the room. "She's sixteen years old O'Grady, how about helping her out a little."

Alisa rolled her eyes. "Yeah O'Grady, jump off of the table and do that funny little Irish dance. You can even give her an Irish accent."

Dan raised his eyes to the ceiling and took a deep breath. He smiled at Carol. "Please, darling, slow."

"Sorry, Dad."

"Okay, back to what you were saying. Someone... told... Warren..."

Alisa began to fidget. *Why is this taking so long?*

Carol kicked it in gear a second time. "That's right, I didn't talk to her, she was talking to Warren, and she told him she talked to Diego and she said he told her he..."

Dan lifted his hand to his daughter's lips. "Please, darling. We need to get through this tonight." He lowered his hand. "Tell me if I understand it so far. Diego's former girlfriend told Warren something?"

"Yes."

"And she heard it from Diego?"

"That's right," Carol said.

"And Warren told you?"

"Yes."

Alisa could not take it any longer. She waved both hands and turned to Carol. "Tell him about killing people!" She gasped and her hand covered her open mouth. "I mean tell Dad who talked about killing people," she mumbled, through her fingers.

Dan patted the couch beside his leg. "Relax, Alisa. You want to sit?"

"Sorry. No, I better stand."

Dan shook his head. "Okay." He looked at Carol. "What did Warren say?"

"He said Diego told his girlfriend he wanted to kill the boys that were calling him Crash."

Dan glanced across the room and stared at the wall for a full five seconds. "When did Warren tell you this?"

"Today, at school."

Dan nodded and took his daughter's hand. "Now, don't get upset when I ask you the next question. A yes or no answer will suffice."

"Okay, Dad."

"Was Ed one of the boys who called Diego Crash?"

Carol's eyes widened and her mouth fell open. "Yes." Her lips trembled and tears filled the corners of her eyes. "Dad, I don't think Diego would kill anyone."

"Perhaps not darling; we'll see. I don't want you to tell anyone what we discussed." Dan put an arm around her. "You'll make a good detective one day. Thank you for telling me."

She hugged her father and wiped her eyes. "You're welcome, Dad. I'll keep it secret." Carol stood, took her mother's hand and pressed against her. She kissed her mother and walked to the hallway.

Dan stepped beside Alisa and put his arm around her. He lowered his voice. "She may have helped me catch a killer."

XVII

PACO

Dan looked at his watch. *Ten PM.* He did not intend to spend all night in Colon. He watched people dodge traffic, from his position near a seedy joint along the bar lined road. Across the street, a spinning nightstick caught his eye. A Guardia Nacional officer stood his post near the corner of a building.

Not far from the police officer, Paco stood in front of a street vender laboring over a small barbecue-stand. A wood fire burned beneath a hubcap, with holes in it, and loaded with unidentifiable meat on a stick. Sweat dripped from the vender's face and sizzled into steam when the drops hit the scalding wheel cover. He wiped his forehead and splashed yellow sauce over the meat. Paco dropped change into a tin can and grabbed a skewer. Rotted teeth clamped shut and dragged pieces of meat into his mouth. He wiped his lips on his sleeve.

Dan dodged traffic crossing the street and walked up behind the man he sometimes called the Night Urchin. "Hey Paco."

Paco spun around and smiled. "The police par-tee tonight?"

"Yeah man," Dan said in his best Bajan accent. "Me, the two tourists and fifty sailors in town drinking and chasing whores. Everyone loves this shit hole. Did you find out anything about the boy killed at Gatun?"

"One day back, me talk wit Chan-see."

"Who's Chauncy?"

"Him is me fren."

"What did he say?"

"Him listen to talk in old Colon."

"About what?"

Paco glanced at people passing, looked at those standing nearby and lowered his voice. "Tu Tu Vieja."

Dan raised his eyes to the night sky and sighed. "What did Chauncy hear?"

Paco leaned in and Dan leaned out. "Her no kill da man."

Dan clenched his jaw. He did not come all the way downtown to find out what he already knew. Paco provided him with good information off the street but often tried to play games. Sometimes he thought Dan should pay him a salary each week for his services. *Not tonight Paco, I'm in a hurry.* He grabbed Paco's faded shirt and spoke through his teeth. "Jesus Christ, Paco. I know she didn't do it, she's a goddamn fairy-tale."

Paco's mouth dropped open, and he stared bug-eyed over Dan's shoulder.

A nightstick tapped Dan on the arm. He turned.

The Guardia Nacional officer, in a tight pressed uniform, smiled. "Buenas noches, señor Dan."

Dan grinned and released Paco's undersized shirt.

"You need my help?"

"No. This gentleman was directing me to one of your fine bars."

The officer raised his eyebrows and pointed his nightstick down the road. "Try the Continental; you will enjoy yourself."

"That's too high class for me, but thanks. Tell Major Noriega I said hello. I'll drop in to visit soon."

The officer's head lowered, he tapped his nightstick against the brim of his hat and stepped away.

Dan took in a deep breath. *Mention the name of the man in power. It works every time.*

Dan straightened Paco's shirt. "OK Paco, she's not a fairy-tale, she's real, I'm sorry." He handed him a five-dollar bill. "Here, give this to your Mom and tell her I send my regards."

Paco stuffed the bill into his stained jeans and flashed a smile.

"Did you talk with any other people?"

"Me hear the talk people say."

Dan pointed to Paco's pocket. "Come on Paco, you've got five dollars of my money. It's getting late and I'll go broke if you keep dancing around this."

Paco looked from side to side.

Why is he frightened? The streets did not become crowded until midnight or later and he had noticed no one out of the ordinary. Those he normally saw staggering between bars must still be inside, working their way to a drunken stupor.

"I think da gringo do it."

Dan nodded and bit his lower lip. *Now we are getting somewhere.*

"Was it someone from the Canal Zone?"

"Yeah man."

"How do you know?"

"Da Obeah woman axe questions."

"About what?"

"Gringos and jaguar fett."

Dan spotted a bargirl staring at him and walking in his direction. Her outfit looked as if she recycled if from a group marching in the Samba Parade at Rio de Janeiro's Carnival celebration.

Dan caught Paco's eye, raised his finger to his lips and faced her. When she smiled, he recognized her from Black Beard's, a raunchy sailor hangout.

She walked up to him. "My barman say give you this." She handed him a worn leather wallet.

Dan opened it, removed a military identification card and looked at the photo of a young sailor.

"Da boy spend all da money, drink all da rum and dat thing jump out da pocket." she said.

"Thank you, I'll give it back to him." He handed her two dollars and winked. "Don't tell the barman."

She shoved the money in her cleavage, spun around and ran.

Dan grinned. *Same old routine. One of the girls relieved the kid of his money, then gave the empty wallet to the bartender and said she found it.*

"Okay, what were you saying?" he asked Paco.

"Ya good to all da people, Mista Dan."

"Sure, a real altar boy," Dan said, figuring it would go right over Paco's head. "Did you hear any names?"

"No man."

"Was it a man or woman?"

Paco shrugged.

"The people you talk to, will they speak with me?"

Paco grinned. "No, yeah crazy man. Them boil you in coconut watta!"

"Anything else?"

"No, me listen Mista Dan. And Mom, her spendin ya money and smilin tomorrow."

Dan nodded. "I'd rather she gets it, and not the other people in town."

###

Dan approached Tierra's door. It opened before he got close enough to knock. The boy stood in the doorway, waved him in and pointed to the back room. Dan bent over, walked through the doorway and stopped inside the room. He turned around and looked at the solid wood door and the windowless wall. A person standing in the room could not see the street. He shook his head, stepped to the back room and parted the beads.

In dim candlelight, Tierra sat at the table wearing the white dress, and the blood red scarf wrapped and tied around her head. Beside her, a stone rested on top of a single folded facial tissue. Dan tightened his jaw and looked at her. *She's sitting there waiting for me to walk in the room. How did she and the kid know I was coming?* He slid out a chair, paused beside it and looked at the paw on the wall.

Tierra spoke with a soft voice. "I am glad you returned."

"May I look at the jaguar paw?"

Tierra nodded.

He removed it from the wall, sat in the chair and placed the paw on the table. "It looks real."

"It represents Tu Tu Vieja to many women in Panama."

"In what way?"

"Their house is protected. Bad men will not enter."

Dan shook his head. "How can they believe something like that?"

Tierra paused and stared at him. "Do you think it is foolish?"

"Yes I do, and I don't understand why people listen to that stuff."

She smiled and raised her eyebrows. "I do not believe in small men who wear green clothing and make shoes for fairies."

O'Grady is no secret, but who told her. Was it Sancha? "You can't compare leprechauns and hidden pots of gold, to claws, a revengeful woman, and murder."

"And so, because we live in different worlds, one light and one dark, your beliefs are more important or more real than the beliefs of the people of Panama?" Tierra asked.

"No, but as I said, I don't understand your beliefs."

Tierra pressed her lips together and nodded. "For the moment you do not, but you will. You and I share something important."

Dan tilted his head and furrowed his brow. He and this woman shared nothing. "That can't be. You said our worlds are night and day apart."

"Yes, they are, but disciples live in the dark and in the light. Look at us, we are both believers." She pointed to the paw. "That beautiful hand of the jaguar is a gift from a friend."

"Where'd your friend get it?"

"She made many and sold them. That one is different from most she made, in two ways."

"How?"

"It is the largest. Now, pay careful attention to the claws."

Dan turned the paw over and examined the three inch long pointed protrusions. *Too perfect to be real.* He leaned over and stared at them.

"Examine your hands and then the claws."

Dan raised his hand and spent a moment comparing it to the paw and its claws. "It's the left."

Tierra nodded. "She made many, but only a few left paws."

Dan's interest piqued. The earlier talk with Paco helped, but his gut feeling told him Tierra knew more than the Urchin's friends on the street did. "I need to talk to the woman who made this."

Tierra pressed her lips together and shook her head. "She cannot speak to you."

"Then you can ask her questions for me."

"Even I cannot speak with her."

Dan had no power over this woman. Tierra did not have to tell him the truth and if he was not careful; she could lead him around in circles. He tapped his fingernails against the table. "Why won't you help me?"

"I do not speak with the dead."

Dan pressed his teeth together. *Slow down, quit assuming things and quit leading.* He fell right into that trap and didn't see it coming. "I'm sorry for your loss. When did she die?"

"Three months ago. She was old like me."

Dan lowered his eyes to the claws. The room fell silent as he slid a finger from the base of a claw to the point and pressed against it. The point broke the skin of his fingertip and he watched a drop of blood fall to the table.

Tierra shifted in her seat. She moved the small stone, picked up the tissue and placed it on top of the drop. Blood soaked into the paper and formed a red circle. After folding the soft paper, she returned it to the same spot on the table and replaced the stone.

Dan looked at her and then to the tissue. *My blood. Why?*

Tierra waited a few moments before she spoke. "You will never find Tu Tu Vieja, few that see her live to describe what they saw."

"Maybe not, but I will find the killer."

"Will that prove she does not exist?"

"No. It's not my job to prove she does or doesn't exist. I'm trying to solve a murder. Someone, and not something, is using a paw like this to kill."

She raised her wrinkled palms. "Now, time for you to learn. How can I help you?"

"Learn what?"

"When you were here last, you told me something important. Why did you say the first one killed was a boy?"

Dan remembered her reaction to the word 'boy' during his first visit. That night he let it pass. He forgot, but she remembered.

"He was seventeen years old."

The words hit a nerve. Her posture stiffened, and she held her breath a few seconds. She closed her eyes, took a shallow breath and opened them. "Tu Tu Vieja does not kill children. Someone evil is hiding behind her."

"That's why I need your help. Can you find out who bought paws this size?"

She glanced around the room and nodded. "Her daughter may know."

Dan perked up and straightened in his chair. "Where does she live?"

Tierra held a hand up in front of him. "Be patient, nothing moves fast in Colon. It is better if I ask. Her mother's work killed a child. Sancha will contact you when I get more information."

XVIII

CHECK IT OUT

Dan drove into the dark parking lot in front of the Gatun Locks Engineering Section, pulled into the manager's vacant parking place and cut the engine and lights.

The door opened a few inches and Juan peered out the small opening. He stepped from the office before Dan got out of his car.

"Got a minute, Juan?"

"Yes."

"You see anyone walking around or fishing along the lake?"

Juan looked at him as if he were speaking Chinese. "Only a crazy person will go near that place." He glanced at his watch. "Almost two AM, I've been in my office for three hours."

"Okay, thanks. Do me a favor, tell your boss to ask the men to keep their eyes open. If they see anyone, call the police station."

"There will not be many calls. No man working here at night wants to turn in that direction. Everybody is afraid that if they see the woman or her lantern, she'll kill them."

Dan nodded. *How can you see something that doesn't exist?* "Tell them not to worry. I'll look around again."

Dan drove from the parking lot to an intersecting street. He stopped, looked in both directions and glanced at the small leprechaun hanging below the rear-view mirror. He tapped it with his finger. "Let's go check it out, O'Grady." He spun the steering wheel of his unmarked Chevy and headed toward the lake.

Turning onto the dirt road, he slowed and directed the beam from his flashlight along the shoreline. The car reached the grassy patch of ground at Parker's Place, and he stopped. The car's headlights illuminated the wall of vines and trees in front of him.

At least five people looked over the area after Ed's death. *Maybe they missed something. I have to take another look.* Dan did not know what he might find. A short walk-around the area would not hurt. *Clues pop up at the oddest times.*

He turned off the engine and lights, got out, and straightened his light police department jacket. Legions of frogs croaking was the only sound he heard. Their clamor smothered all other noises of the night. He looked around and purposely slammed the car door. The frogs did not miss a beat. Whatever they were screaming about, was more important than his interruption.

At the jungle wall, he took short steps along the fringe of the dense vegetation, moving his flashlight between the thick growth and dark grass in front of him. His stomach quivered. Snakes loved frogs, and Dan feared three types of snakes; big ones, little ones and dead ones. A slow boa constrictor didn't worry him; they weren't venomous. The most feared snake in Panama, the two-inch fanged Fer-De-Lance liked the night. One swift strike of the large viper could cost a body part or his life. The damp grass looked as if it may be their favorite place to hide.

Dan continued a short distance and noticed the silence when the frogs suddenly ceased their nighttime song. *They know something I don't.* His eyes and beam of light darted across the face of the jungle. He turned around and squinted at his car.

Dan couldn't explain what happened next. Call it a premonition, instinct, luck, a feeling, or whatever. Muscles tightened and a flush of adrenaline shot through his body. His eyes widened with alarmed recognition and he spun toward the dense thicket.

A black paw with three-inch claws lashed out from the jungle foliage and struck his left arm. The claws ripped his jacket tearing into his flesh.

Years of training and practice governed his movement. Dan dove and rolled to the side. He came up on one knee, drew his automatic and fired three shots across the face of the jungle.

XIX

STITCHES

Alisa, wearing pajamas and a short robe, squeezed her fingers around the coffee cup. She passed through golden rays of early morning sunshine flowing in the windows of the living room. Pacing around the rattan furniture, and silently wishing O'Grady would do something, had not helped. Dan was not a person to work all night after making a single telephone call home to say he was busy. *Must be a development in Ed's case.* The sound of a car approaching the house broke her thought pattern. She suppressed a need to step out and greet him at the top of the stairs and waited for him to walk through the door.

Alisa froze at the sound of a knock on the windowless door. *It's not Dan.* Her hand shook as she eased it open. Ralph's robust frame filled the doorway. With wide eyes and teeth clenched, she grabbed his arm. Her voice shook. "Where's Dan?"

He pointed to the bottom of the stairs.

"He's okay... he's with you?" she asked.

"Yeah, he's getting stuff out of the car."

Alisa let out a breath and her muscles relaxed. "What stuff?"

Dan trudged up the steps and Alisa focused on gauze and tape wrapped around his left arm. A line of blood stained the wide bandage that covered his upper arm. In his right hand, he carried a large white paper bag. Alisa's hand covered her open mouth and her eyes glanced from Dan to Ralph and back to Dan. Carol stepped beside her mother and gasped at the sight of her father's arm.

"Hi, babe."

"What happened?"

Ralph stepped into the house and Dan lowered his head and entered.

Alisa reached for the bandage but Dan flinched before she touched him. "I wasn't paying attention and had an accident."

"A car accident?"

"No, I was up at Gatun Locks."

Ralph pointed at the bag in Dan's hand. "The hospital sent bandages and iodine. Make sure he keeps it clean."

"How bad is it?" Alisa asked.

"It's nothing," Dan glanced at Ralph.

Ralph looked at Alisa and turned to Dan. "Twenty-two stitches is nothing?"

Alisa's fright turned to anger. "What the hell did you do to yourself?"

Dan ignored both of their questions and pointed to her coffee cup. "Ralph, want coffee?"

"No, I'm meeting Lou."

"Fishing?"

"Yeah. Make him rest, Alisa."

"I will." She hugged Ralph before he slipped out the door.

Alisa pointed to the couch. "Sit down and relax, I'll get you a cup of coffee."

Dan watched his wife walk to the kitchen. *How am I going to explain this?* He plopped on the couch beside Carol, poked the bandage with his index finger and examined bloodstains seeping through the gauze.

"Does it hurt?" Carol asked.

"A little. Are you going to school?"

"I was, but maybe I should stay home."

"I'll be fine, you better get going."

"Are you sure?"

"Yes. I'll be here when you get home."

Carol kissed him and walked to the kitchen.

Alisa came out of the kitchen carrying a coffee mug. She sat on the couch, handed him the coffee and studied the hospital's work. "Okay Detective Smartass, the truth, what happened?"

Dan stared at the floor. Alisa knew him well. Many times, Mr. Smartass turned into Mr. Hardass. If he attempted to deceive her, she would discover it in no time.

"I went up to the locks to talk with a guy. When I left I went by Parker's Place. I was standing near the jungle where Ed died."

"Why?"

"To make sure no one was fishing or hanging around. Everyone knows to stay away from there."

Alisa's eyebrows rose. "Okay, and then what happened?"

"I walked along the edge of the jungle and suddenly it became quiet."

"Quiet? What do you mean?" Alisa squirmed in her seat.

"When I arrived and got out of the car, every frog within a mile was croaking. I couldn't hear any other sounds. Then, near the jungle, total quiet. For some reason, the frogs stopped making noise, and the area seemed empty. Silence surrounded me and I sensed something."

Alisa's voice shook, and she stiffened. "Sensed what, damn it?"

A quick glance at her eyes told him she was frightened. Often, when she and her mother told stories of witchcraft and black magic she would become uncomfortable, but he had never seen this look of terror on her face. "I don't know, just a feeling. I turned toward the jungle and what I saw was a black paw and claws tearing into my arm."

Alisa recoiled and gasped. She grabbed his uninjured arm. "You saw Tu Tu Vieja." Her hands trembled as she pulled her knees up in front of her chest and hugged them. Her gaze lowered to the floor, and she rocked back and forth.

She is frightened to death. He placed a hand on her knee. "Come on Alisa, I saw no one."

She lowered her legs and turned to him. "It was her, I know it."

"Babe, it may have been a cat."

Wide eyes locked on his. "How big was it?"

"Who knows? Like I said, I didn't get a close look."

"Did you hear it growl?"

"No."

"If you didn't, then it was Tu Tu Vieja!"

Dan looked at the leprechaun figurine on the table across the room. "Does that make any sense to you, O'Grady?"

Alisa leapt to her feet and headed toward the telephone. "Don't start that shit with the stupid little gold hoarder!"

"Who are you calling?"

"My mother, she'll figure out what to do, she can even..."

Dan stepped up and stopped her. "Please, not this morning. I don't want potions to drink, powders to throw in the air or feathers to pin to my drawers."

"She'll know how to keep you safe," Alisa said, wiping a tear from her eye.

Dan could not ask for a better mother-in-law. No one in Panama put together a better meal, was as caring or as generous. Her lone fault was to leap into action the second her daughter showed signs of distress and asked for her help. *The wrestler, Man Mountain Dean, would not stand a chance against her.*

Dan kissed his wife's cheek. "I'm sure she'll have a few suggestions, but please talk to her later. When you do, ask her to light a candle and say a prayer."

XX

MARIE

Marie walked into the Knights of Columbus and looked at Ollie. The meat cleaver stood upright in the counter behind him. She spotted Diego and headed to his table.

During the holidays and summer breaks, she left Baton Rouge to enjoy time with her family in the Canal Zone. This trip was different, she did not want to leave her friends at LSU and miss a week in New Orleans with her sorority sisters. *Wish Dad had not asked me to come.*

When she reached Diego's table, she pulled out a chair but did not sit. "How long you been here?"

"Five minutes."

"What do you want to eat?"

Diego shrugged. "Cheeseburger and coke is fine."

Marie turned toward the bar. Everyone spoke Ollie's language. "Ollie. Two hamburga cheese, one big fench fi, big coke, one tea ice."

"You pay dollar twenty five cent," Ollie yelled.

"No problem," she said, flashing him the OK sign and sliding into the chair.

"Where were you yesterday?" Diego asked.

"Me? You are the one who's been a ghost. When I came home, I wanted to spend time with you but you're never at the house. I went to a racket ball tournament on the Pacific side."

"What am I supposed to do, plan my schedule around your vacation?"

Marie tightened her jaw and drew in a breath. "Great vacation."

"Did you play in the tournament?"

"No, just watched. I wanted you to go, but couldn't find you."

"Must have been doing something," he mumbled.

It was obvious he was not in the mood to answer questions. Gathering her thoughts, she studied him a moment. Since the terrible accident that left the scar, he had put up a barrier between himself and everyone else in the family. After she arrived home, her father warned her of Diego's short temper. "Were you with someone?"

Diego looked at the table and sighed. He grabbed the saltshaker, poured a generous amount on the table and attempted to balance the glass shaker on its edge. When he succeeded, he looked at Marie. "I need to be with someone? Why did you want to meet me here?"

I have to break through his shell. "Mom said you were helping Mrs. Walker."

"Yeah. What does she have spies watching me?"

Marie turned to look at Ollie. She slowed her breathing and inhaled to calm herself. Turning, she glared at her brother. "Why are you punishing yourself? Can't you stay away from those jerks?"

"They don't bother me."

Ollie yelled across the bar. "Hamburga cheese, fench fi, pay money now."

Diego walked to the bar, dropped a dollar and a fifty cent piece and picked up the food tray.

"You pay too much, one quarter," Ollie said.

"You work too much, Ollie. Keep the twenty five cents," Diego said. He returned to Marie and slid the tray on the table.

"Listen. You know I worry about you?" Marie said.

He avoided eye contact. "I'm a big boy I can take care of myself."

"I wish you had more friends."

"You left three years ago. I have friends and I stay busy."

Her attempt to discuss the problem ended in frustration. She shook her head and grabbed a handful of fries. "Heard anything about Ed?"

"Carol told me her dad is trying to find out what happened."

"Carol Casey?" she asked.

"Yeah, her dad is the cop."

"What did she say?"

Diego smiled. "He doesn't believe in Tu Tu Vieja."

"There's something out there and I don't want to run into it."

"It's probably a big cat."

"Think they'll find it?" she asked.

Diego stared at her and shook his head. "Cats are smart."

XXI

THE BOOKKEEPER

Dan sat in the living room and held Carol's three ring binder full of lined paper on his lap. A pencil eraser rested against his lips. The eraser slid into his mouth and he chewed on the pink rubber.

Alisa walked into the room and looked at the two dirty plates, napkins, and an empty mug on the coffee table in front of him. "What you doing?"

He lowered the pencil, ripped a page from the binder and closed it. "Writing questions that need to be answered."

"About what?"

"The two murders that are driving me crazy... been sitting here all day. I don't enjoy waiting for other people to dig up information for me. The woman you sent me to see in Colon will help, but I can't wait forever."

"Relax and let your arm heal."

"After all these years, you know me better than that," Dan said. "Ever see me warm my ass on the couch all day?" He stood. "Help me change this bandage before I go out."

Alisa tightened her jaw, and she placed both her hands on her hips. "You're not going anywhere tonight."

Dan did not like defying Alisa, but the investigation was too important. He walked into the Fantasy Bar at ten that night and looked at the crowd. Smiling girls preyed on happy patrons while the jukebox belted out calypso sung by the Mighty Sparrow. On his way across the room, an empty stool caught his eye; he pulled it away from the bar and sat. The bartender looked up, nodded and pointed at the bandage on his arm.

"It bruk?"

Dan shook his head. "No, just a small cut."

"Gringo or island man do it?"

"Not a man, an animal."

The bartender mixed a strong, dark, rum and coke. He slid the drink in front of Dan and placed the rum bottle next to it. "Wit pain, rum is me fren."

"Thanks," Dan said pouring more rum into the glass. "Is Sancha working tonight?"

The bartender tilted his head toward a door across the room. "Her in back. Dat door beside big man, room on da left."

Dan glanced around and spotted his large quiet friend sitting in a dark corner. He grabbed his drink, dropped a bill on the bar and headed to the door.

The glaring single light bulb hanging above a flimsy table forced Dan to squint. Sancha sat at the table digging through a stack of receipts. The slit in the long colorful sarong around her hips exposed her olive-toned leg and thigh.

"They make you the bookkeeper?"

"I'm the only one who finished school," she said, staring at his bandage. In one smooth motion, she stepped to him and gave him a cautious hug. "What happened? Does it hurt?"

"It's sore."

"Did you get shot?"

"No, cut."

She shook her head and wagged a finger at him. "Too many people in Panama have knives. Did you forget?"

"It wasn't a knife."

"What was it?"

"Claws."

Sancha tilted her head, giggled and placed her hands on her hips. "Gringos and their jungle pets. Was it a coati or a cute little jaguarundi?"

"Bigger."

It took a second for her brow to furrow and eyes flick from the bandage to his face. "Was it a puma?"

"No, the paw and claws of a black jaguar."

Sancha raised her eyelids as her dark eyes stared into his. "Have you told Tierra what happened? She came to see me and we talked."

"Ula? No, I've said nothing to her yet."

She glanced around the room. "How do you know her name?"

"The same way she knows my life story."

Sancha reached out and touched his uninjured arm. "We can help you."

"Good, she wanted to see..." Dan halted mid-sentence and sipped his drink as he took a moment to consider her words. "We? Why did you say we?"

"My grandmother was Ula's friend."

"So?"

"She made the jaguar paws."

Dan's mouth dropped open. "Your grandmother?"

Sancha nodded and smiled. "For many years, she sold them."

"So it's your mother Tierra wanted to contact?"

"Yes."

"Did they talk?"

"Not yet."

"Did Tierra tell you what she and I discussed?"

"Yes." Sancha crossed the room and picked up a cloth bag. She removed a large jaguar paw matching the size of the one on Tierra's wall. "A paw like this one."

His eyes widened. "How many big ones did she make?"

"Only six this large, but she made many sizes." She handed it to him.

Dan turned the paw over and studied it. "Were all of them left paws?"

"No. Three left and three right. One left and two right have not been sold."

Dan calculated. "Ula has one on her wall. Who bought the other two?"

Sancha grinned. "I don't know, but I'm sure my mother would remember."

Dan visualized the next few steps of his investigation. If Sancha's mother knew who bought them, he would be closer to finding the killer. "Good. I need to talk to her."

Sancha stalled and wet her lips. "You can't, she won't speak to you."

"What do I have, bad breath?"

Her eyes narrowed. "I don't understand."

"No one wants me to ask my own questions."

"They offend the spirits."

"Come on Sancha, it's not about spirits."

Her lips pressed together, and she glared at him. "My mother believes in them," she said sweeping a hand in front of him. "No one can change that."

Dan took a deep breath and exhaled. He reached out and touched her cheek. "I'm sorry, I'm learning. Ask her if she remembers who bought them."

"When she returns, I will."

"Returns?"

"She's visiting family in the interior."

"I'm trying to solve a murder." He thought a moment. "Call her."

"It's a small village, they don't have telephones."

"When is she coming home?"

"Maybe tomorrow or the next day."

Dan lowered his head. "Should have listened to my mother."

"Your mother?"

"She told me to be a priest."

Sancha could not stop her grin. She kissed his cheek. "Then we wouldn't be friends."

Dan tapped her on the ass. "Trying to get me in trouble?"

"I can't, Alisa would be angry."

He removed a wad of cash from his pocket, unfolded two large denomination bills and handed them to her. "Buy yourself a nice sexy dress, something to make the rich guys go crazy." He hugged her. "Call me after you speak to her."

Sancha winked, slid two fingers inside the slit of her sarong and exposed her thigh. "Why are you leaving?"

"I've got my hands full right now."

She released the garment and looked into his eyes with a serious expression. "Do you know what my mother would say?"

"No idea."

"The lady watches you, but you will not see her."

Dan believed everyone in Panama was watching him stumble through the investigation into the two deaths. People in the Canal Zone had one opinion; the locals had another and the Guardia Nacional did not give a damn because the murders happened on territory under the jurisdiction of the American government. No one wanted to hear his theory. Nothing less than solid facts would bring them together. He tilted his head and grinned. "Your mother is correct, Sancha. Haven't seen her yet, but I will. And when I do, she will go to jail."

XXII

THE GYM BAG

Dan, with his hands under his chin, sat at his refinished wood desk. A wood framed photo of O'Grady hung on the wall behind him.

Ralph walked into the room holding the large jaguar paw and a file folder. He slid into a chair. "Your arm any better?"

"Yeah. Thank God it wasn't deep."

"Read your file." He dropped the folder on the desk, stared at the spot it had landed and slid the folder to the side. "Damn, the desk top looks good, when did you finish?"

"Last week, before all this started."

"What did you use on it?"

"Stain and rubbed it with oil for hours."

Ralph held up the paw. "You saw what those claws did to your arm." He raised the paw. "Don't let this scratch up your work."

Dan nodded. "I won't."

"Things are beginning to make sense but a crap load of questions need answering," said Ralph. "One thing is bothering me. How would someone get a good grip on this and swing it hard enough to do that much damage?"

"I don't know. What I saw looked as if it may have been a cat's leg, not just a paw someone or something held in their hand."

"Doc's report said he identified left and right paw marks on both bodies." Ralph swung the paw in front of Dan. "No way you can hold it, much less two of them, and tear apart a person's throat and chest."

"We'll figure it out."

"When you going to interview Diego?"

"This evening, over at Cristobal High. The kids in Millie Walker's class are organizing the school's annual talent contest. She scheduled a get together with them tonight. Diego will be there."

"Wish we could tail him."

Dan shook his head "Too much open space, we'd get burned."

Ralph gazed at the floor and nodded. "Think I'll go with you tonight."

Dan sat with Ralph and a group of parents at the back of the recently painted classroom. Every other classroom in the school had tan walls. Millie's were light blue, and she had scattered many large potted plants around the room. She did things her way, and no one dared complain.

Small groups of students spread themselves out across the room. Dan chuckled. Each had positioned their group a safe distance away from the others. *They have their own little cliques.* Steve, Frank and two friends sat at student desks along a wall opposite the open windows. Another group, in hard wooden chairs, formed a line against the long windowsill on the wall across from them. Other students, occupying desks, surrounded Carol, Katy, and Warren, in the middle of the room. Millie Walker sat erect, at a large desk in front of the class.

Dan glanced at Diego, in a chair beside Millie's desk. The large scar, disfiguring his face, drew his eyes to it. The traffic officers that interviewed Diego after the accident had described the gash, but Dan did not realize it started at his forehead, crossed his eye, and ended at his chin. He shivered. *Must be rough living with that on your face.*

Carol turned toward her father and caught his attention. She held up a locket, on a gold chain around her neck, and grinned. Dan smiled and nodded his approval.

Mrs. Walker stood. "Is the decoration committee ready?"

"Yes," Steve said. He removed a black gym bag from the desk and set it on the floor.

Mrs. Walker looked toward Carol and Katy. "Katy, has your group completed the list?"

"Not yet."

"We'll take a short break to give you time to finish."

Katy's father, the Chief Customs Inspector, entered the room and walked to Dan. "Forgot to turn off your parking lights... checked the door, it's locked."

"Thanks." Dan leaned to Ralph. "Be right back."

Dan stepped into the dim, empty hallway, marched to a large door at the end of the hall and shoved it open. A musky smell hung in the stale damp air of the stairwell. He bounded down the flight of stairs. On the ground floor, he thrust both hands against an unlocking bar on a steel door leading to the parking lot. The door flew aside, and he bumped into a petite girl in shorts and a T-shirt. His head jerked back, and he smacked his left arm against the doorframe. He moaned and grabbed the arm.

"Damn it," he said. The girl in front of him looked familiar but he could not attach a name to her face.

She stepped back and looked up at him. "Did I scare you, Mr. Casey?"

"No, I should have taken my time." He studied her face. "You're Diego's sister?"

"Yes."

"Marie, correct?"

"That's right."

Dan nodded. "Nice to meet you." He pressed his hand against the bandage on his throbbing arm.

"We met a few years ago."

Dan studied her a moment. "Yeah, that's right, I remember now."

Marie looked at his bandage and frowned. "What happened to your arm?"

"I cut it at work."

"I hope you didn't hurt it again when you bumped into the side of the door."

"No, it's okay."

"Do you see my brother upstairs?"

"Yes, he's sitting up front with Mrs. Walker. How's he doing?"

Dan noticed her muscles tighten. Her brow creased, and she let out a short breath. "He's good, why?"

Being alone with Marie provided him with the perfect opportunity to ask a few questions. Her uneasiness told him she was not comfortable. He paused hoping she might relax. "I was wondering how his recovery went. I understand he's mad. Two of the kids upstairs were laughing at him."

Marie cocked her head to one side, her eyes narrowed. "I wasn't here when the accident happened. I don't think those boys were ever his friends. They're punks. Diego can take care of himself. Excuse me." She slid past him. "See you later."

That was quick.

On his way back to Mrs. Walker's room, Dan pondered Marie's demeanor. She stuck up for her younger brother, just as he had years ago for his brother. He couldn't blame her. Carol was his only child, but if she had a little brother, he would expect the same. He had noticed Diego's physique. *He doesn't look as if he needs anyone's help.*

Dan returned to the classroom and saw Marie in the chair he had occupied next to Ralph. She looked at him, smiled and tipped her head toward an empty chair on the opposite side of Ralph.

"Have you finished, Katy?" Mrs. Walker called out.

"Yes."

"Give Diego the list, he'll put them in order of performance."

Dan heard a snicker. He glanced at Diego, glaring at Steve and his friends.

Marie looked at him with a 'see what I mean' expression.

"Everyone go to the auditorium. We have twenty things to do, and I want to be finished by ten-thirty," Mrs. Walker said.

Dan leaned to Ralph. "Let's talk to him, and then we'll head back to the station."

They stepped to Millie's desk and Dan leaned over and whispered. "Excuse me, Millie; we need to speak with Diego."

"Don't keep him long." She stood and walked out of the room.

###

At ten fifteen, Steve, Frank, Carol and Katy left the building and walked toward cars in the well-lit parking lot.

Steve stopped. "Damn."

"What?" Carol asked.

"My gym bag is in Mrs. Walker's room."

Carol shrugged. "So? You can get it tomorrow."

"I can't, my house keys are in it." He turned to Katy and Frank. "I'll be right back."

"I'll go with you," Carol said.

They turned around and headed through the stairway door. When they reached the dim and deserted second floor hallway, Steve stopped.

Carol stared at the long passage. "I've never seen it empty and dark. It looks spooky."

"Why don't you go with them? Tell Ollie to make me two hamburgers," Steve said.

"Okay, hurry." Carol headed down the stairs.

A motionless figure crouched in the shadows at the front of the dark classroom. Its eyes turned as the door opened and Steve entered. The figure watched him look toward the chairs and walk to his gym bag lying under a desk. He hesitated, stared at the bag and then attempted to drag it from under the chair with his foot. A strap, wrapped around the desk's leg, prevented the bag from moving. As he leaned over to raise the desk leg, a faint shadow crept over him. Steve stood and turned.

A black streak slashed toward Steve's face. His eyes widened with terror but the figure gave him no time to react. Claws ripped his throat open and blood sprayed across the wall.

XXIII

THE LOCKET

Early Saturday morning, Dan sat at his desk reviewing his case file. He could not take his mind off Paco's statement that a gringo bought the large paws.

Ralph stepped into the office wearing civilian clothes. "You working all weekend?"

"No, just going over a few details. I thought you were going fishing with Lou."

"Tomorrow. Did you hear from your informant's mother?"

Dan stood and sat on the corner of his desk. "Yeah, it somewhat surprised me."

Ralph dropped into a chair.

"A Panamanian boy bought two large paws. She didn't know him, but remembered selling them. He said they were for a gringo."

"Man or woman?" Ralph asked.

"She didn't ask."

"When did she sell them?"

"Sometime last month, but couldn't remember the date. And he bought a piece of hide she had dyed black."

Ralph's forehead furrowed, and he stared across the room. "For what?"

"Who the Christ knows."

Manuel tapped on the doorframe.

Ralph turned to him. "Yeah, Manny."

"Commander, Dan." Manny looked at a note. "Arlo, a janitor at the high school called. He said he saw blood on the hallway floor."

"So?" Ralph said.

Manny raised his eyebrows. "He sounded frightened, his voice shook."

Ralph turned wide eyes to Dan. "I sure hope it's a kid's sick prank."

"Didn't sound good, sir." Manny said.

Ralph and Dan headed to the door.

"Dan will ride with me. We'll follow you, Manny."

Ralph, Dan, and Manuel turned into a hallway on the second floor of Cristobal High School.

Arlo leaned against a wall and trembled. He wiped sweat from his face and neck.

"I'm Captain Philips. Where did you see the blood?"

Arlo pointed down the hallway. "That way, near the end."

"In the middle of the floor?" Dan asked.

"No, in front of Mrs. Walker's door."

Ralph looked at him and nodded. "Did you go in the classroom?"

Arlo's eyes bulged, his mouth hung open. "No. I didn't even want to wait here for you, but the man on the phone told me I couldn't leave until he arrived." He walked away. "I'm going home."

"Wait, Arlo. What's your last name?"

"Lopez."

Ralph turned to Manny. "Stay with him."

"You can't leave just yet. Stay with Officer Cabrera, he's the one you talked to and he'll make sure you're safe. Detective Casey and I will take a look."

Ralph and Dan approached Mrs. Walker's classroom and spotted a small red circle on the floor below a blood stained doorknob. Two thin red streaks led toward the stairway door at the end of the hall. They paused and looked at each other.

Dan pulled his pistol from his waistband, shoved the classroom door open, and slipped inside the room. He scanned along the walls and spotted the body. Ralph pushed past him and they stepped to the prone figure. Blood pooled on the floor under Steve's throat and chest.

Ralph squatted. "Jesus... Mike Bruno's kid. His brother-in-law is Commissioner Harrison. We're in trouble now."

Dan turned toward the door. "I'll find a phone and call Doc Lopez."

"Hold on a minute, what's this." He pointed to Steve's chest. "It's woman's jewelry. Wonder who owns it?"

Dan leaned over and saw the locket. His pulse raced. A sudden coldness passed through his chest. "That's my mother's."

Ralph thrust his car keys to him. "Take my car."

XXIV

WHERE IS CAROL

A hundred different scenarios passed through Dan's mind as he drove home to check on Carol. The first one he cast aside was calling Alisa. Early that morning when he left the house Carol was in bed. *Please let her be home.*

The car skidded to a stop in the driveway below the house. Dan leapt out and bolted up the stairs. On the landing, he noticed a white cup with a piece of paper covering the top. *Someone left her drink out here.* He ignored it, rushed into the house and slammed the door.

His muscles tensed and he scanned the living room. "Alisa!"

Her voice came from the hallway. "Yes, what?" She dashed into the room holding a pillowcase.

"Where's Carol?" Dan realized he should have calmed the tone of his voice. It took Alisa seconds to show her concern. Her hands trembled.

"Why? Katy picked her up two hours ago. What's wrong?"

Don't lie to her. His breathing slowed, and he looked around the room. "Where'd they go?"

Alisa moved close to him and focused her wide eyes on his. "They went to meet Steve and Frank on the old pier at Fort Sherman. She took one of your fishing poles."

"Did you let her wear my mother's gold locket?"

Alisa pressed her lips together and took his hand. "Yes. Tell me what's wrong!"

Dan pulled her close to him. "Carol's friend Steve is dead."

Alisa blinked three times and squeezed his hand. "Steve Bruno? What are you saying?"

"This morning we got a call from the janitor at the school. When Ralph and I got to Millie's classroom, we found his body. Mom's locket was lying on his chest."

"Mother of God," Alisa gasped and her knees yielded to the weight of her body. Dan grabbed her before she fell. "Come on, pull yourself together. I don't know why he had the locket or how it got there but we need to find Carol, now." He pulled her toward the door.

He held Alisa's hand and guided her out of the house. When she stepped onto the small landing, her foot slipped. She looked down and screamed.

Dan clamped his arms around her waist and held her. His eyes widened and locked on the overturned cup and a puddle of blood on the concrete pad as he lifted her off her feet. *What the hell? Whose blood is that?*

The car's brakes locked. It plowed through gravel, and stopped beside a Jeep, at the front of a wooden pier jutting over clear emerald water. Dan and Alisa jumped out and spotted Katy and Frank fishing at the end of the pier. They ran to the two teenagers.

"Where's Carol?" Dan asked.

The kids looked at each other with raised eyebrows.

"What's wrong?" Frank asked.

"She went to get Steve," Katy said.

The expression on both their faces reminded Dan of a frightened victim. He did not intend to raise their concern to a point of panic.

"Last night she told me she was going to the KC with him. Did she?" Dan asked.

Katy shook her head. "No, he went back to Mrs. Walker's room to get his keys. Carol came with us. He said he'd meet us there. Everyone was tired, and when he didn't show up, we thought he went home."

Alisa looked at the jeep at the end of the pier. "How did she go to get him?"

"She took my car, about fifteen minutes ago," Katy said.

Dan turned to Frank. "Is that your jeep at the end of the pier?"

"Yes."

Dan looked at Katy. "Were you driving your father's old Chevy station wagon?"

"Yes."

"Was she going to Steve's house?" Alisa asked.

Katy nodded. "I bet he's still sleeping. Is everything okay?"

"Steve isn't at his house, he's hurt. I want you to leave now and go home." Dan said. He took Alisa's hand. "Go with them."

Alisa clutched her arms across her chest. "No, I'm going with you."

Katy and Frank shot puzzled glances at each other.

The only road between Ft. Sherman and Gatun Locks stretched over ten miles through jungle and marsh along Limon Bay. If he drove fast enough, he might catch her before she crossed the locks. He needed to find Carol and make sure the two apprehensive teenagers in front of him remained safe.

Dan pulled Alisa close to him and whispered in her ear. "Someone needs to speak with their parents and tell them what happened." He kissed her and stepped back. "I'll catch up with Carol. If you don't see me by the time you reach Gatun, I'll meet you back at our place." He took off toward the cars. *It always happens at night... please let it stay that way.*

Dan dove behind the wheel, gunned the engine and fishtailed away from the pier.

He remembered seeing three cars heading to Gatun on his way to the pier. He pressed his lips together. *I'm a cop. I'm supposed to remember things I see.* He shook his head.

The white knuckles of his hands caught his eyes. He loosened his grip on the steering wheel as he blew through a stop sign. Jungle and damp wetlands lined both sides of the two-lane road. When he reached ninety miles per hour on a straight section of roadway, he eased his foot from the accelerator and watched the black pavement race under the wheels. The open space below the rear-view mirror reminded him he was driving Ralph's car. *Hope his tires are in good shape.* Had he been in his Chevy, O'Grady would be hanging from the mirror. He shook his head and focused on the road. "Help me out O'Grady. Please let her be okay."

After the second murder, he should have placed restrictions on her. Two teenagers were dead, and both were her friends. They hung around with the group of kids that Diego hated and even admitted he wanted to kill. *He cooperated, but I need to check out what he said.*

The car reached a right-hand turn and Dan released pressure from the gas pedal. A coatimundi dashed across the road. The brakes dropped the nose of the car and it skidded to the shoulder before he regained control. "You little bastard," he muttered. He shoved the gas pedal against the firewall, climbed to sixty miles per hour and lifted his foot to set up for a curve. Dan knew if ships were going through the lower locks, Carol would have to wait to cross the narrow bridge across the canal. The car accelerated out of the curve.

The Chevy station wagon sat on the side of the road with a flat tire. All the windows were down and the passenger side door was open. Dan slammed his foot on the brake pedal and skidded past the car. *Where is she?* He spun the unmarked patrol car around, stopped inches from the bumper of the station wagon and jumped out.

He scrambled to the open passenger door and surveyed the interior. A Styrofoam cooler lay on its side in the back seat. He kneeled on the front seat, reached over and up-righted the cooler. A large rat scurried from it, jumped to the floor and leapt out the open door. Without thinking, he shoved himself away from the seat, slamming his back against the dash. "Son of a bitch."

It wasn't like Carol to leave the car and walk along a road bordered by jungle and salt marsh. The taste in his mouth turned sour and his heart raced as he stepped from the car and searched for footprints leading to the jungle. He let out a sigh of relief when he saw none and headed to his car. "Thank God."

Dan pulled around Katy's car and gunned the engine. His brow furrowed and teeth closed on his upper lip. He looked into the rear-view mirror. "I came this way... think dummy!" He made a quick U-turn and sped toward Gatun Locks.

Mangroves and trees flashed past the car but he focused on the pavement in front of him. Carol would remain his only child. He and Alisa would never forget the moment the doctor told them they could not have more children. *If something happens to Carol, it will kill Alisa.*

At a curve, Dan tapped the brake pedal. Halfway through the curve he shoved the accelerator to the floor and saw Carol standing in the grass with her thumb out. He took a deep breath and moved his foot to the brakes. *Thanks for watching her, O'Grady.* The car slid past her. Dan jammed the shift lever into reverse and the tires screeched. The car stopped beside his daughter and he jumped out.

Carol's wide eyes locked on her father. Perspiration sparkled on her skin and damp clothes clung to her body. She flinched as Dan ran up to her.

"Damn, you scared me," he said.

Her lips and chin trembled. "I'm sorry. What's wrong?"

Dan looked at her bare neck. *How did Steve get the locket?* "What happened to Grandma's locket?"

Carol reached to her bare neck and gasped. Her mouth dropped open and tears formed. Her voice cracked. "I... I don't know."

Dan put his arms around her. "Don't worry about it now. I came looking for you because Steve's hurt."

She freed herself from his grip and raised a hand to her lips. "How bad, is he okay?"

Dan placed his hands on her upper arms and squeezed. "No, I'm sorry darling, he's not."

He tightened his hands the moment she fainted.

XXV

THE TARPON KING

Three days after Steve's murder, the early morning sun hovered low in the sky over Gatun Lake. Lou stood fishing in an open area at the edge of the water near Parker's Place. A holstered 38 Police Special hung from his belt. A wooden stake poked from the ground and an open bottle of beer stood next to his feet. Parachute cord, tied to the stake, led to a bait bucket floating in the lake. He filled his lungs with warm damp air and watched a large crocodile glide past the half-submerged bucket. *Don't screw with my bait, big guy.*

The rumble of an approaching car caught his attention. Dan's Chevy parked beside his old truck. He stepped from the vehicle and removed a custom fishing pole from the back seat. "Catch anything yet?"

"No keepers. Should have tried for snook or tarpon at the spillway."

"Got any bait?"

Lou pointed at the bucket, bobbing five feet from shore. "It's loaded with good-sized shrimp."

Dan pulled in the bucket and grabbed a fat, wiggling shrimp. He removed the hook from a guide on his pole, impaled the pink crustacean and cast into the water. "Glad you're carrying the 38."

"Me too, a damn big crock went by a few minutes ago."

"Was it a caiman or crocodile?"

Lou raised his eyebrows. "Too damn big to be a caiman." He watched Dan reel in his line and examine the fidgeting shrimp before he cast back into the water. He shook his head and tried not to let Dan see the grin on his face.

"Still have your two-man cayuco?" Dan asked.

"Yeah, it's over at the Gatun Yacht Club. Use it every week."

"You keep an old cutout log at the yacht club?"

"Why not? I pull it up on the grass... everyone knows it's my boat."

Dan grinned. "You don't rent a spot at the dock?"

"Don't be a wiseass."

"Want to help me catch Tu Tu Vieja?" Dan asked.

Lou reeled in his line and grinned. "Got bait?"

"I gave Carol the job of laying the ground work."

"How?"

"I suggested a cookout; she'll sell the idea to the kids."

"Where?"

"Right here."

Lou froze and stared at him. "You nuts?"

"A little dangerous, but not crazy. It'll be in the afternoon and parents will chaperone."

"What's the plan?"

"Meet me and Ralph for a drink later today... at five o'clock. Ollie is back on the warpath. He may throw that thing."

"The meat cleaver?"

Dan nodded and smiled. "Yeah."

Lou shook his head. "Been swingin it for years, he ain't thrown it yet."

Dan reeled in his line; the shrimp had won its freedom or met its doom. He placed the hook over a guide and cranked the line taut.

Lou shook his head and raised his free hand. "One and a half casts and you're leavin?"

Dan stared at him. "What the hell does one and a half casts mean?"

"The first one didn't count. You yanked that poor little bastard out of the water before he had time to get wet."

"Hell. I reeled him in the first time to find out if the water was cold. He said it wasn't." He swung his pole as if casting. "I don't want to show you up by catching the big one."

Lou pressed his lips together to keep from smiling. "Ya think you can out fish the tarpon king?"

"Another day, your highness. Don't forget, the KC at five."

After her dad asked for help, Carol called Katy and Warren and suggested they meet. As they walked inside the Cristobal Yacht Club, they saw Diego sitting alone and joined him at his table.

Carol, Katy, and Diego sat overlooking the water and the pleasure boats tied to the docks. Warren walked to the table and set two large bowls of French fries and two small bowls of melted butter in the center. Everyone grabbed fries and sloshed them through butter on the way to their mouths.

"I can't believe people are being killed. My parents won't let me go anywhere alone," Katy said.

Warren leaned forward. "When Steve was killed at school, people said it may not be Tu Tu Vieja."

"It had to be," Diego said.

Katy shifted in her seat and stared at him. "I thought she was at Gatun and had a cayuco and a lantern."

"Yeah, how could she get to the school?" Warren asked. "It's a long way from the lake."

Diego placed both his arms on the table. "I was in Colon earlier and heard people talking. They said she can go anywhere."

Katy shrugged and shivered. "How does she move from place to place?"

"The same way ghosts move around," Diego said.

Carol glanced at everyone and leaned against the back of the chair. "We need to plan something... a cookout. It would be to honor Ed and Steve."

The others at the table stiffened and looked at her.

Katy's mouth hung open, and she blinked. "What do we have to celebrate, two dead friends?"

Carol shook her head. "Not celebrate. We need to let their families know we care and show respect."

Diego took a deep breath, lowered his head and focused on a bowl of butter.

"Maybe we can plan something at Piña Beach," Katy suggested.

Warren moaned. "That's a long way and the parents won't drive that far."

"Why not up at the locks?" Carol asked.

"Are you crazy?" Katy asked.

Warren shook his head and glared at Carol. "That's where Ed and the old man died. Your dad said it was off limits."

Carol held up a hand. "Not at Parker's Place, closer to the canal. I heard my Dad tell his friends it was okay to go fishing there again."

Diego tilted his head and his eyebrows formed a shallow V. "Is the investigation finished?"

"I think so. He said they may never find out who did it."

"Better to have it at the locks, it's closer than Piña," Warren said.

"What day should we have it and what should we do?" Katy asked.

"This Saturday may be a good day. We can ask a few people to bring charcoal grills. We'll get our parents to buy the food," Carol said.

Diego slid his chair back and stood. "They weren't my friends, count me out."

XXVI

THE DUNGEON

Dan sat at a table in the Knights of Columbus. He stirred his glass of rum and coke with a finger and eyeballed Ollie and Ralph at the bar. Ralph, on a stool, held a bottle of Pabst Blue Ribbon beer in one hand and his chin in the other. He listened to Ollie and tried to slide a word into the one-sided conversation. Ollie held the meat cleaver at shoulder level. It moved in unison with his rambling, inaudible speech.

Dan smiled at the animated conversation and looked around the room. The other patrons, evening regulars in the bar, were not interested in Ollie's rant or the chopping movements of the blade inches from his bald head. Dan often said he ran the bar as if it was his private establishment. Selected people received short shots for the listed price while others collected strong drinks. The few on Ollie's good guy list paid the price he whispered across the bar.

Dan looked at the two men. *Ralph's frustrated.* While Ollie controlled the conversation, Ralph's head bounced from side to side and he pointed at the large knife. The bottom of his beer bottle tapped against the bar and he thrust a hand in the air.

Ollie didn't skip a beat, his mouth and sharp weapon continued to move.

Dan watched Ralph shove his index finger at the liquor bottles, lining the top of the cabinets against the wall, and mumble something to Ollie.

Ollie stared at him while his free hand raised two dripping beer bottles to the bar. His eyes did not move from Ralph as he brought a glass of ice up from under the bar and reached back to snatch a bottle of dark rum from the counter. With one hand, he opened the bottle, and half-filled the glass. *How can he be so efficient with one hand and control that meat ax with the other?* Ollie screwed the cap on the bottle and returned it to its place behind the bar.

"Wow." Dan shook his head. *I can't believe it. I could watch him for hours.* "He never took his eyes off Ralph and didn't even blink."

Ollie lowered the meat cutter to the bar but kept his hand over the handle. From under the bar, he lifted an open bottle of coke and poured an ounce into the glass of rum. He slid the glass beside the beers.

Ralph slapped three bills on the bar, grabbed the drinks and headed to the table.

Ollie smiled, slipped two dollars into his shirt pocket, and drove the tip of the cleaver into the back counter.

Duly impressed, Dan locked his eyes on the large upright blade and did not move them until Ralph set the drinks on the table and dropped into a chair.

"You and him must go back quite a few years?"

Ralph smiled. "I was a young cop when he became the bartender." He slid the rum to Dan and placed a bottle of beer in front of an empty chair. "The kids are driving him nuts. They all come in at once, order a bunch of hamburgers and pay for half of them."

"I was here the other day when one tried that. Whatever you said made him happy."

Ralph lowered his head and raised his eyebrows and eyes to Dan. "I told him I'd put them in the jail's underground dungeon."

Dan smiled and nodded. "That's the humane thing to do. Otherwise, he removes a few of their body parts."

Dan and Ralph looked at Ollie and laughed.

"He's harmless," Ralph said.

Lou, wearing cutoffs and a T-shirt, strolled to the table and sat in front of the full beer.

Dan looked at the words on his shirt, 'Fish, Fish and Beer'. *It's Lou, it should be 'Beer, Beer and Fish'.*

"What's so funny?" Lou asked Dan.

"Ollie's ready to do surgery."

Lou studied the men sitting at tables scattered across the floor. "Who's the patient?"

"The kids," Ralph said.

"Ralph convinced him he'd put them in balls and chains and lock them in the jail dungeon."

Lou glanced back and forth between both men. He turned and looked at Ollie's trusted chopper imbedded in the counter behind the bar. "Looks safe, for the moment." He grabbed his beer and took a sip. "Where's the dungeon?"

Ralph and Dan burst out laughing.

"Assholes. What's the big plan?" Lou growled.

Ralph could not remove the grin from his face. "Got a good idea, it may end our murder mystery."

"Remember, I told you Carol was going to suggest a cookout?" Dan asked.

Lou nodded. "Yeah."

"Well, she passed the word around that the open area near the spillway side of the locks isn't off limits anymore."

"The kids know?"

"If she did her job they do and hopefully they're planning the party as we speak."

"What can I do?"

Dan scooted close to the table. "We need your big cayuco. Our asses will be out on the lake."

"Who's gonna back us up?"

Ralph tapped the table with his fingers. "I'll cover it from shore with Manny."

XXVII

JUST LIKE THEY SAID

Clouds obscured the stars and moon. Lights at Gatun Locks sparkled like fireflies on the polished black surface of the water. The flickers stopped at the wall of dense jungle along the shore.

Dan and Lou, in dark clothing, paddled the large two-man cayuco. Lou sat in the back. Behind him, a double-barreled shotgun lay on a faded orange life vest. The cutout log boat coasted to an unlit buoy and Lou tied a line to a metal support beam.

"We better keep it low, sound travels over water," Dan whispered.

"It's spooky out here at night," Lou said.

"The lake doesn't scare me. It's sitting in this little boat, eight inches above the water, and wondering how big the bastard is that's lurking below the surface... now that frightens the shit out of me."

"Couple of days ago a local guy hooked into a twenty footer north of Escobal... about six miles from here."

Dan turned and looked at him. "Don't start with the giant reptile stories, Lou. Those crocs love Yankees, especially Yankee meat from Boston."

From the buoy, the men had an unobstructed view of the shoreline and jungle next to the locks.

"We may get lucky. This afternoon that place was assholes and elbows with people. There must have been thirty kids... sure hope they all left," Lou said.

"Ralph took care of it. He and Manny chased everyone out before sundown."

"Ya think this plan will work?"

"It should if the killer thinks a few of the kids are still there. Ralph will have a case of red-ass if it doesn't." Dan squinted at distant movement on the lake. He turned to Lou, raised a finger to his lips and pointed across the water.

The faint image of a single figure, in a small dugout canoe, glided across the lake.

"Could be someone fishin," Lou whispered.

"We'll see."

They watched the figure take intermittent deep strokes and guide the craft toward the jungle at Parker's

Place. The faint glow of a lantern appeared at its bow. A twinkle of light shimmered across the water making its way toward land.

Dan felt a tap on his back. "Yeah?" he whispered.

"Looks like the locals said it would."

"What?"

"The Lady of the Lantern."

"Don't tell me you think that's a four hundred-year-old woman?"

"I don't, but someone wants me to believe it's her."

What the hell? Not long after Ed's death, Dan doubted a jungle cat or an old woman had anything to do with the kid's death. Everyone knew large jaguars were not this far north, but he and Lou were the only people who would admit it. *Someone is playing games.*

"Untie us, keep quiet," Dan said.

Lou pushed the boat away from the buoy and they eased their paddles into the water.

"Go toward the open area where you were fishing," Dan said.

They watched the small dugout reach shore, and the lantern go out. A shadowy form disappeared into the bush.

When they were thirty feet from land, Lou tapped Dan on the back and pointed to shore.

Motionless, on the sand near the edge of the water, a twelve-foot long crocodile turned its head toward them. The giant raised it heavy body from the ground and hauled itself to the lake. Silently slipping from shore, the reptile disappeared below the black surface.

Their bow pushed onto shore at the spot the crocodile had vacated.

"Keep the flashlight off," Dan whispered.

Dan and Lou stood and inched onto solid ground. Lou cradled the shotgun, a flashlight poked from his back pocket. Dan held his 45 automatic in his right hand and a flashlight in the left. His stomach churned and chest tightened. He motioned for Lou to follow him.

They crept along the border of the dense growth. Dan stopped, pointed at Lou and then to the ground. Lou nodded and froze.

Dan continued along the line of vegetation. He looked back at Lou and pointed his unlit flashlight toward the jungle. Lou slipped his flashlight under the front grip of the shotgun and released the safety on the weapon.

###

A dark shape squatted in thick groundcover and cloudy haze coming off the warm water. Two large paws rested on the damp ground. Five sharp claws protruded from each paw. It gazed back and forth. The only sound was its own breathing. It crouched lower to the ground at the sound of movement. Two streams of light suddenly illuminated the undergrowth on its left and right.

The dark shape alerted at the sound of footsteps and the sight of approaching lights. It turned and dashed toward the water. Limbs, leaves and squatty palms slammed into its body until it reached the edge of the lake. Forty feet from shore, the small cayuco bobbed in the water. The figure sucked humid air into its lungs. It glanced toward the oncoming lights, spun and leapt into the lake.

Dan heard the commotion in the water. "Quick! Run back to the boat!"

Dan and Lou raced from the jungle and headed to the small beach. Lou leapt into the back of the boat, set his shotgun on the life vest and gasped to catch his breath. He lifted his paddle as Dan shoved them off the sand and jumped aboard the small craft.

Dan looked back at Lou. "Head toward the splashing." He wiped sweat from his face and forced his paddle deep into the water. The bow turned toward the turbulence.

The empty boat, drifted sixty feet in front of them. Dan caught sight of the massive crocodile when it broke the surface halfway to the small craft. The giant glided in the same direction they paddled, the same direction as the elusive figure thrashing in the water ten feet from the drifting cayuco.

"Jesus, that thing is getting close," Lou said.

"Damn," Dan yelled, watching the reptile slip below the surface. "Whatever that thing is, the croc will tear it to pieces."

The water around the figure erupted. The crocodile thrashed, spun and pulled its victim below the surface.

They stopped paddling and surveyed the dark water. *We're too late.* In the silence, Dan could hear the rapid beats of his heart and Lou's heavy breath.

"That croc is big," Lou whispered.

"We'll be lucky if we find anything," Dan said.

"Let's tie-up to that boat and get the hell out of here."

"We can't," Dan said. "I need to see if we can find anything. Whatever that thing was, it killed three people. I want an answer."

"Christ Dan, be careful. This little boat won't frighten a croc that big. He'll come out of the water to get to us. Keep your pistol ready."

Two thoughts flashed through Dan's mind. Late night dinner for an ugly reptile was not a part of his plan. *Maybe the meal he had filled his belly.* Lou was right. If that monster wanted them, they had no chance in the flimsy canoe. His second thought bothered him the most. He turned, looked at Lou and raised his eyebrows. "Whatever you do, Lou, don't point that scatter gun in this direction."

Dan splashed water on his face, lowered his paddle into the lake and took a slow soft stroke. The paw of a jaguar shot from below the surface and embedded its claws into the top of the sideboard next to him. Both men rocked away from the large claws.

"Holy Jesus!" Lou screamed.

Claws sank into the soft wood and their boat tipped toward the water.

Dan looked back at Lou. "Keep us upright!"

Lou's half dollar size eyes locked on the paw. He shifted his weight in the opposite direction. "Hit it!"

Dan reached below the paw and grabbed an arm of black fur. Pain from his injured left arm shot across his chest. "Don't let us capsize." Favoring the right side of his body, he struggled to raise the figure's arm.

"What the hell ya doin? Get your 45," Lou said.

Dan turned and saw Lou leaning over the far side to keep them from flipping. His head and shoulder rested inches from the water; his bleak expression framed in horror and fear.

"Hurry! That bastard comes up he'll remove my head!"

Dan clamped his teeth together, took a deep breath and yanked the arm.

A woman's face broke the surface. Dan jerked his head back and froze. Marie's wide ghost-like eyes locked on his. *My God, it's Diego's sister.* She gasped for air.

Dan pulled her halfway over the side of the cayuco. Her head rested against his leg. She wore a black shirt and tight black pants. He could not see her hands. Black fur covered both her arms from her shoulders to the large jaguar paws. He glanced at Lou. "Help me."

Dan kept their boat level and Lou grabbed Marie's thigh. He pulled her body over the side and into the boat. The stump of her severed leg landed in his lap. Blood spurt from an artery onto Lou's pants and chest. He cringed and raised his head. "God, she's dyin." He turned his head and dry heaved.

"Jesus, we have to get her to shore quick." Dan raised his 45 above his head and fired two shots into the air. Red flashing police lights came on and a police cruiser sped toward the nearby shore.

XXVIII

SHE ROAMS THE JUNGLE

Dan took Sancha's hand, parted the beads leading into Tierra's back room, and led her to the candle lit table.

Tierra, in a black dress with her red scarf wrapped around her neck, sat in a chair across the table from two vacant wooden chairs. "Come, sit. Good to see you Sancha," she said in a soft voice.

"You look good, Aunt Ula."

Tierra smiled. "You have always been my favorite, how is your mother?"

"Good, she prays you are well."

"I am." She turned to Dan. "Your arm gets better each day?"

Dan nodded. "It's nothing. I'll be fine in two or three weeks."

Tierra extended a hand toward his left arm. "Give me your hand." With a touch as gentle as a grandmother, she placed a hand on his bandage and closed her eyes. She raised her hand to hover over the bandage and looked into Dan's eyes. "Twenty two stitches. The little shoemaker was at your side."

Dan struggled to cover his uneasiness as he glanced at Sancha and saw her hiding a smile.

"Alisa and Carol?" Tierra asked.

"They're fine."

Tierra brought her hands together and her fingertips touched her chin. "I heard you found the killer."

Dan nodded. "With your help."

Tierra paused. "She still roams the lake."

He furrowed his brow and tilted his head. "No, she died at the hospital."

The old woman's eyebrows rose, and she shook her head. "The killer you found died at the hospital, Tu Tu Vieja did not."

Dan strained to smile. "I respect your beliefs. Speaking with you helped me solve three murders." He leaned toward her and grinned. "O'Grady and I thank you."

Tierra laughed. "A spirit and a fairy. Both hiding in their solitary worlds until needed."

Dan stood and motioned to the paw hanging on the wall. "I want to show you something." He brought the paw to the table, sat and pointed at the end opposite the claws. "If you open this end, you'll notice Sancha's grandmother filled it with newspapers held together by glue. The killer removed enough paper to make a space for her hands, so her fingers extended to the claws. She then added more paper and glue to make the paw stiff."

"No one should steal the beliefs of my people," Tierra said.

Dan shook his head. "I don't think it will ever happen again."

Tierra nodded, took Sancha's hand and passed it to Dan. "I hope one day this beautiful child will no longer work in a bar."

Dan tapped Sancha's hand. "Then both of us must help her."

Tierra smiled. "You're a good man, Detective Casey."

XXIX

O'CASEY

Students and parents gathered for another barbecue in an open area beside Gatun Locks. Carol and her friends stood near smoking kettle-shaped grills, loaded with hamburgers and hotdogs. At the water's edge, Dan and Lou stood next to a cooler filled with ice and beer. Both held fishing poles and beer bottles.

"Now ya know more about Tu Tu Vieja than the locals," Lou said.

"I still don't understand parts of the story but I figured out why they believe it."

"What ya mean?"

Dan took a short swig of beer. "Women are home alone and need something to make them feel safe. They look to an old story passed down for generations. They are told if they keep a fake jaguar paw in their house, it will protect them."

Lou grinned. "Like my friend the cop, lookin for help from a little green man."

"O'Grady?" Dan asked.

"Ya mean you gave him a name?"

"I didn't give it to him, but he's got one."

Lou nodded and rubbed the stubble on his cheek. "I guess everyone swears by somethin crazy." He smiled broadly. "An old friend told me if I keep a beer in my hand, no harm will ever come to me."

"That may be true... seems to be working. But it's sad when someone preys on superstitions to hide a murder."

"Ya goin soft on me?" asked Lou.

Dan threw an arm over Lou's shoulder. "You don't have to worry. But if I ever show-up with flowers, instead of beer, you'll know everything has turned to shit."

Jim strolled up behind Dan. "Catch anything, Mr. Casey?"

"Yeah, Moby Dick's little brother," Dan said.

Lou turned to him and tilted his head from side to side. "Okay, O'Casey."

Lou's right. Quit being an asshole. "Sorry Jim. We haven't had a bite."

"Old tarpon king saying," Lou said. "Get your ass out of bed early if you want to catch the big one."

Dan raised both arms in front of him and bowed twice. "Yes, Master Lou."

Jim looked at the cooler. "Got any beer?"

Dan smirked. "Ice cold, you're old enough, go ahead and take one."

Jim grabbed a beer. "Thanks. Good luck fishing." He walked away.

Captain Phillips walked up to Dan and stuck his hand out. "Good work. Glad I have a detective that sees things from another perspective. We'll keep you around for another fifteen years." He turned to Lou, tapped him on the shoulder and grinned. "And it's an honor to have an old retired friend who hasn't seen the dungeon yet."

XXX

A LANTERN GLOWS

Juan strolled to the end of the lock at the edge of Gatun Lake. He gazed at anchored ships waiting to drop the level of the Atlantic Ocean. Their lights reflected off the water's mirror surface.

Next to him, mechanical mules tightened cables attached to a laden ship. Electric motors whined when the mules inched forward, guiding the ship past colossal doors and into the lock.

They caught the murderer but this place still scares me. After a minute staring at the black water and dark jungle, he walked away from the lake.

An odd feeling came over him. He stopped, turned, and looked over the water.

Beyond the stern of the ship, thick dark jungle surrounded the still ebony surface of Gatun Lake. In the inky distant, the faint glow of a lantern appeared. The flicker of its light inched across the water. It reached shore and disappeared into dense jungle foliage.

THE END